# Diablo –
# A New Home

Gabi Adam

# Diablo –
# A New Home

*For everyone who cares about horses*

# Chapter 1

Thirteen-year-old Ricki Sulai was just as crazy about horses as most other girls her age. She would spend hours with her friends Cathy and Lark at the riding academy, while their teacher, Mr. Bradford, got gray hair over their bad grades at school.

Then, last Christmas, everything changed.

"It's amazing what a horse can do," Ricki's father marveled when he saw his daughter pouring over her schoolbooks and notebooks without his prodding.

"Well, not everyone has a four-legged tutor," Ricki responded happily, as she shoved various folders into her backpack and slung it over her shoulder. "I'll do math in the stable. Kevin has to explain something to me," she said, picking up the basket with Diablo's grooming equipment and wedging it under her arm.

Giving her father a quick peck on the cheek, she hopped on her bike and started off for the Bates farm, where Diablo and several other horses were being stabled until new stalls could be found for them.

Ricki pedaled hard, impatient as she was everyday, to see her horse. She was thankful that Diablo was still alive,

5

given the terrible fire that had completely destroyed the riding stables some weeks before.

"Hey, Ricki! Hello! Stop! Wait up!" Kevin came racing up to meet her on his bike. As usual, the two of them had planned to get together in the late afternoon after school. Without setting a time, somehow they always managed to meet at the fork in the road leading to the Bates farm.

"Hi, Kev, what's up?" Ricki beamed.

The boy grinned. "I've been shouting and waving at you for a while, but you're obviously on another planet today."

Ricki shrugged her shoulders. "Sorry, I was just lost in my thoughts."

"What? You can think?" he teased. "I would have never expected that of you. . . "

But even before Kevin had finished speaking, Ricki had reached behind her into the grooming basket on her bike carrier, found the large sponge, and threw it at Kevin's head. "Oh, I seem to have dropped something," she said sweetly.

Kevin flashed her an oh-don't-play-Miss-Innocent-with me look, then picked up the sponge and handed it back to his girlfriend. Ricki thanked him with a gentle kiss on the cheek. She was always happy when Kevin was around.

In the last six months a very tender, close relationship had developed between the two young people, and they enjoyed every minute they could spend together.

"I was just thinking about how the riding academy burned down all because of Lark and Cathy."

For a while, the two of them rode silently side by side lost in their own thoughts.

Everything had begun shortly before last Christmas. That was a time that was to alter Ricki's life entirely.

Frank Cooper, a wealthy member of the riding club and

sponsor of its annual tournament, had often mistreated his horse, Diablo. Ricki, who had been at the stables and witnessed one of these incidents, had tried to stop the man from abusing his horse. In his anger and rage Cooper had struck her with the horse's bit. Jake, the old stable master, had come to her aid, but had been unable to prevent her from collapsing with a broken collarbone and waking up later in the hospital.

Jake, who had actually raised Diablo, was eventually able to buy the black horse for the symbolic price of one dollar from the animal-protection group that took charge of him after Cooper's abuses became known. He had decided to give Diablo to Ricki both as a present to help her overcome the horrible experience and as motivation to improve her school performance. In addition, he was convinced that in Ricki's care, Diablo would be in the best possible hands.

And that's what happened. At Christmas, the teenager became the proud owner of the black horse. Diablo made her the happiest person on Earth, and Ricki promised herself to study more and to do well in her classes so as not to disappoint Jake or her parents, who had approved this fabulous gift.

Unfortunately, Cathy and Lark became envious of their friend, who now spent a great deal of time with her horse and her boyfriend, Kevin. Kevin Thomas was also a classmate of Ricki's and often helped her with math, her worst subject, and also with the care of Diablo, whom they both loved. Kevin was allowed to ride Diablo, but the two girls were not, and this really upset them. They began a campaign to make Ricki's life miserable. Soon she was being shunned by many of her friends at school as well as at the riding academy because of the lies Lark had spread about her. Then Lark and Cathy secretly began riding Diablo and Doc Holliday, Cathy's favorite horse, after dark. One night the oil lamp that they used as their light to saddle the horses was kicked over by accident, setting the entire building on fire.

"I still don't understand how anyone could be that dumb," Kevin said, shaking his head and maneuvering his bike around a large boulder.

Ricki nodded in agreement. "I don't understand it either. When I think of what could have happened to Jake, it makes me sick."

The elderly stable master, who lived in an apartment above the stalls, was awakened by chest pains and had called his friend Marcus Sulai, Ricki's dad, for help. Stumbling down the stairs to open the stable door and wait for Marcus and the EMS team to arrive, Jake had surprised the two intruders. But they were able to flee quickly through a defective outer wall.

Jake had collapsed upon seeing the fire, and Diablo remained saddled and waiting in the stable corridor.

Fortunately, Ricki, Marcus, and the EMS doctor arrived just in time to free Jake and the horses with the help of Diablo, who had broken in the heavy entrance door from inside with his hooves.

The police investigation exposed Lark and Cathy as the perpetrators.

After that, Ricki and Kevin felt only contempt for the two girls. Ricki couldn't believe that she had been so mistaken about her girlfriends' characters. Gradually though, their anger focused on Lark because she continued to defend her and Cathy's actions.

Cathy, on the other hand, was very ashamed of her behavior. She was sorry she had allowed Lark to turn her against Ricki. But this insight came too late to change what had already happened, and so Cathy had to suffer the consequences. Nevertheless, she was very glad that no one had been injured in the fire. The worst part for her was the guilt she felt about Jake. She believed that she and Lark caused Jake's heart attack, which almost killed him. Luckily the EMS got him to the hospital in time, where he spent several weeks recovering.

"I think it's really great of your parents to let Jake live with you," said Kevin, as they approached the driveway to the Bates farm.

"Yeah," agreed Ricki. "Jake has really settled in well at our house. He's like family. I can't remember how it was before he moved in." The events of the past few weeks scrolled past her inner eye like a film.

After the stable master had lost his apartment and all his belongings in the fire, Marcus and Brigitte Sulai, who had become fond of Jake even before he gave their daughter his beloved Diablo, were determined to take him into their home.

Jake had settled in with the Sulai family very quickly, taking the place of a grandfather for Ricki and her young brother, Harry. They loved to sit together with Jake and listen to his stories about his life on the horse farm where Diablo was born.

Right before their eyes, Diablo became a foal again, black as night, swaying on wobbly legs, and constantly thinking of new tricks to get the attention of the two-legged ones who took care of him.

Ricki's heart always beat faster when Jake told stories about Diablo. Little by little, he filled in the gaps in the

9

background of her wonderful horse, and she realized that Jake had given Diablo all the love he was capable of while raising and training him. One day, overcome with appreciation, she stood up and hugged the old man spontaneously.

"Oh, girl, save that for your horse," he said, embarrassed, before the mischievous gleam appeared in his eyes. "Or for Kevin," he added with a grin.

"Exactly!" confirmed Harry, racing behind Jake's armchair for safety before he continued. "They have already kissed! I saw them with my own eyes. Ow!"

Ricki sprang at him and wrestled him to the floor. She still didn't like it when her little brother teased her about her friendship with Kevin. She often felt hurt by Harry's teasing and insensitive comments, even though he meant them to be funny.

"Don't let it upset you," Brigitte Sulai said to her daughter. "Little siblings are delighted when they can annoy their older brothers and sisters. You know that. He really has no idea what he's talking about."

"I'm not so sure about that." Ricki stuck her tongue out at Harry and resolved to ignore his comments in the future. However, since her father and Jake had also made teasing remarks whenever Kevin picked her up, she decided that it must be something in the male genes and, that as a woman, she should stay above it all and not feel she has to defend her friendship with Kevin all the time.

"So what's happened to Lark and Cathy?" Jake stretched his stiff back before he leaned pleasurably back into the old armchair.

Ricki let go of the squealing Harry and sat down crosslegged on the carpet in front of Jake.

"Well, Cathy is the personification of a bad conscience.

In class, after they all found out what the two of them were up to, everyone has been giving her funny looks. Her parents have grounded her for an indefinite time. Sometimes I feel really sorry for her," Ricki said pensively.

"And Lark?"

"Lark? It seems her mother and father totally flipped out when the police told them that their daughter, along with Cathy, had sneaked into the stables at night, stolen the horses and ridden them, and was also responsible for the fire. Her parents were so ashamed that four weeks later they moved away with their whole family."

"So," the old man said, looking Ricki straight in the eyes, "and how have you decided to treat your former best friend, Cathy, in the future?"

Ricki shrugged her shoulders. "Honestly, I haven't the slightest idea! She would never have had the idiotic notion of riding Diablo and Holli at night by herself. Lark told Cathy that she wouldn't be her friend anymore if she didn't go along with it."

"Hmm...that's what I thought. What do you think? Could you forgive her?"

Ricki looked down at the carpet and didn't answer. But Jake pressed on through her silence. "Thank heavens, nothing happened to your horse or any other animal."

"Yeah, but you..."

"Me? What about me? I had a heart attack, which I would have had even if there had been no fire."

Ricki looked at him in amazement. "Does that mean you aren't mad at her?"

Jake looked at the photo of Diablo on the wall next to the door. "No, I'm not mad at her." He said slowly. "After all, I'm still alive."

11

"But your apartment, your belongings!"

The old man smiled. "Everything can be replaced, except for life itself – hat's the most valuable gift that we have. And this gift, along with Diablo, has not been taken away from me. In addition, I'm happier living with your family than I was before. So why should I be angry with your friend?"

"My friend?" Ricki asked quietly, and Jake nodded at her.

"Of course! She was your friend and she will stay your friend! Deep down you know that, and that's why you feel sorry for her in spite of everything. You just need a little time to let your heart see it. If you want my advice, be glad that your horse is alive and give Cathy a chance. Her conscience is punishing her enough for the fire so that she will never forget. And if everyone is avoiding her at school, she could really use a friend right now, someone to stick by her despite everything. Remember how happy you were to have Kevin when all of your classmates turned against you?"

"Yeah, but I didn't set fire to any stables."

"That doesn't matter now. Just remember how it felt...the feeling that you had a friend."

Just then, Harry laughed out loud. "Ha! Friend – that's a good one. Kevin's coming today. Can I go with Kevin? Kevin is so *sweet*!" he taunted.

"Harry, shut up and go away! You don't understand anything!" Ricki grabbed her brother by the shoulders and ushered him out the door.

Then she turned back to Jake and began to smile. "Thanks, Jake. I think I understand what you're telling me."

12

"Well, that's great. I knew you would." Then he closed his eyes and dozed. As Ricki tiptoed out of the room, quietly closing the door behind her, Lupo, the old stable tomcat, jumped into Jake's lap and rolled himself into a ball, just like in the old days. There was nothing better than a cozy nap in the afternoon.

*

"Hey, you two, how are you?" Lillian Bates was just coming out of the barn dressed in dirty overalls and armed with a manure fork as Ricki and Kevin parked their bikes in the yard.

The three waved gaily to each other.

"Are you finished already, or can we help you?" asked Kevin, glad that Lillian had forgiven him for having that accident with her horse, Doc Holliday – or Holli, as they all called him.

"A little help is always welcome. When several horses are together in one big stall, there is more to clean up than if they were in separate stalls. In addition, they mess up all the hay so, if you really feel like helping, there's always something to do."

"We'll be right there," said Ricki. "I just have to see Diablo."

"Yeah, I know. I'll expect you guys in two hours in the hayloft."

"Idiot!" Kevin grinned and pushed open the lock on the barn door. The unmistakable smell of horse stalls reached them.

"Ah, I love this smell." Ricki took a deep breath of the warm air before the two of them went inside and closed the door.

All the horses raised their noble heads at the noise and were watching with curiosity as the two walked toward the stall. Diablo whinnied loudly as he recognized his owner. Excited, he started to move toward Ricki to greet her. He kept bumping her and rubbing his forelock on her shoulder until Ricki lost her balance and landed on her bottom.

"Shoot!" she yelled, and Kevin doubled over with laughter.

"You can say that again!"

"Bull's-eye," responded Ricki with fake desperation, before she got up out of the fresh and still steaming horse manure.

"Do you have a problem? I thought you loved him."

"All right, all right! Hit me when I'm down."

In spite of her damp bottom and the odor, she hugged her horse happily around his neck. Watching them, Kevin had a moment of nostalgia for his dead horse, Leonardo. Although he had sworn never again to become attached to another horse, he had to admit that he felt a longing to have a horse of his own again. He wanted to be greeted by a four-legged friend, to stroke him, to care for him and do for him, and to be able to give him all the love, security, and safety that was humanly possible.

Kevin was a little shocked to realize that the picture of Leonardo in his mind had begun to fade, and recently he had to think hard in order to remember exactly how the horse looked. He would never have thought it possible, but since getting together with Ricki and becoming more and more involved in caring for Diablo, it had become clear that Leonardo was never coming back to him and that his life would have to go on. But Ricki had been right when she told him that a life without horses was impossible for him.

Yes, she was definitely right. He would be able to remain true to the memory of Leonardo even though he became attached to a new horse. Someday he would own another horse, one that he could love as much as he had Leonardo, and he would gallop over fields and meadows, feeling the freedom of the wind, and he would be happy again. Just as happy as Ricki was with her Diablo.

"Are you dreaming?" Ricki brought him back from his reverie. "If we stand around much longer, Lillian will have been right about her two hours. Is something the matter? You look so strange."

Kevin shook his head and smiled. "No, no! Everything's fine. I think I feel better than ever. I think I'd like to have a horse again."

Ricki cheered softly, clapping her hands, and Diablo backed away three steps, a little startled by her sudden change in behavior.

"That's awesome! I knew it! I knew it wouldn't be long before you got the itch again!" She gave him a quick, enthusiastic hug. "You don't know how happy that makes me," she said. They stood facing each other, a moment of complete understanding passing between them. Then, hand in hand, they left the barn to look for Lillian.

The fact that Kevin had finally overcome the death of his beloved Leonardo made Ricki forget for the rest of the day that she needed her friend to explain a math problem. But how important was math compared to the wish for his own horse?

*

"And now, ladies and gentlemen, may I present the unbelievable, the phenomenal Rolanda and her beautiful horses.

15

Enjoy this unique equestrian presentation!" Sandro Piccore, alias Henry Jenkins, owner of the small Montollini Family Circus, bowed to his audience, but they applauded his introduction with little enthusiasm. Oh well, what could you expect from approximately 25 spectators.

Life was sad for traveling circus people.

"We can perform only in small towns," explained Sandro, who thought that the name Sandro Piccore was more appropriate for a circus owner than Henry Jenkins, and so also adopted an Italian accent for his performances.

The other family members appeared under assumed names as well. Ann became Rolanda; Chris, Piotr; Marlene called herself Chantal; and Rita was Natasha. One single family managed to represent five nations by their names alone.

"That makes it sound like an excitingly good circus and gets us more spectators than we would get using our own names. Just imagine how boring it would be, if I said: 'Here comes Rita with her gigantic snake.' That wouldn't thrill anyone. But if I introduce Natasha with her slithering beast, which becomes as tame in her hands as a little lamb, that increases the tension and the curiosity about a black-haired Russian woman who, unafraid, wraps a giant boa constrictor around her body."

To keep it simple, and also because they were used to them, the family called each other by their stage names. Therefore, that evening after the performance, when they all gathered in Sandro's wagon, Chantal asked, tapping her forehead, "Tell me, Sandro, are you naive or are you just shutting your eyes to our real situation? The fact is, we are dead broke. We don't even have enough money for the basics anymore. The tent has holes in it and gets the spectators wet when it rains. The benches need to be freshly painted so that the audience doesn't get splinters in their backsides; the music equipment is broken; and we've been using the same costumes for five years; they're so worn thin they can't even be patched."

Piotr nodded in agreement. "She's right, Sandro. Do you think it makes any difference if you introduce Rita as Natasha? The people couldn't care less. They only care about what they get to see for their money."

"But unfortunately, every large circus, with its exciting attractions, is better than us. Why should people attend our performances if two weeks later a Ringling Brothers or a Big Apple circus comes to town?" Rolanda said, completing her husband's thought.

Sandro rolled his eyes upward. He had heard this argument too many times before.

"I have told you this often enough. Only rural towns would turn out to see a small circus like ours, and the inhabitants are as interested in seeing Montollini as they are a cow on a trapeze."

For a moment there was a heavy silence in the wagon.

"I don't want to make it sound worse than it is," Rolanda began cautiously, "but, well, our feed is almost gone. I've been rationing the hay for about four weeks, but I can't give the animals less than I have been giving them as it is. You can almost see Sharazan and Rashid's ribs. I've been using the long tasseled blankets during the performances so that no one notices how thin the horses are."

"Yeah, yeah, I know, I know! But can anyone tell me what I should do?" Frustration showed on Sandro's face. "Should I try to sweat hay and straw from my ribs? Or meat for the lion? Should I give him the boa to eat? Darn it,

17

I've been thinking about it day and night, but we've been in a slump for too long. We can't keep hoping that some sympathetic farmer will give us a few bales of hay or straw for free, or a grocer will give us some old bread, or...or....or..."

The others finally realized that Sandro, the head of the family, didn't know what to do anymore. Nor did they themselves have any idea how to solve their financial situation.

"Perhaps we could sell something," Piotr suggested.

"If you don't *have* anything, you can't *sell* anything," answered Rolanda.

"Well, maybe Sharazan or Rash–"

"Are you crazy? Those two are the best part of the show! And I would never give either one of them away. They are my life! Sell your lion – the only thing he can do is growl." Once more, as so often in the past, Rolanda asked herself why she had married this man.

"Horse maid," snorted Piotr, full of contempt. "It's still better to growl than to be carried around."

"If you are referring to the boa," Natasha snapped, angrily getting up, "you can forget it. I– "

"Children, stop bickering, this isn't getting us anywhere. We have to come up with something else." Sandro rose, opened the door of the wagon, and, with a nod of his head, motioned them to leave. "Now, let's go to bed. It's late, and we have to leave early in the morning."

Sandro watched as they all walked back to their wagons. Then he closed his door as well, turned off the light, and fell back on his bed exhausted. He stared at the ceiling in the darkness. The last thing that went through his mind before he fell asleep was Piotr's suggestion. If they sold one of the animals they could buy feed for the remaining ones.

But regardless of which animal they sold, it would mean one less attraction. It was a vicious circle.

*

Lillian, Kevin, and Ricki sat together on the bales of hay, which were stacked up in the back of the barn. The horses had been taken care of and the sounds of pleasurable chewing filled the temporary stall.

Kevin, his head resting against a wooden post, nibbled on a piece of straw as he daydreamed. In his mind, he saw a large roan, similar to Leonardo, but with an even shinier coat, a nobler body. In short, Kevin's dream horse was similar to Diablo, but with one difference: Ricki's horse was black.

Lillian leaned back and observed her Doc Holliday with devotion. The ligament he injured when he accidentally stepped in a hole while Kevin was riding him was finally completely healed. "Man, I can't tell you how glad I am that none of the horses were injured in the fire."

"Hmm," said Ricki before she got up to go over to Diablo. She wanted to avoid any more thank-you speeches, which Lillian already had delivered three times within the last few weeks.

In the weeks since the fire, each of the horse owners had called Ricki and her father to thank them for saving their animals. Diablo had received pounds and pounds of carrots and apples for the large part he had played in it. After all, he had broken down the door, allowing the animals to escape from the burning stable. Ricki distributed the carrots and apples evenly to all the horses in the Bates' stable.

"The article about you and Diablo in the animal protection society's magazine was great, by the way!" Lillian grinned. "Do you feel any different as Animal Protector of the Year?" she asked, and Ricki groaned and rolled her eyes.

"Of course I feel different," she answered. "What do you think it's been like since the magazine came out? They printed pictures, stupidly, and people are always asking me, 'Hey, are you the girl, who…?' 'Oh, that's the girl with the miracle horse…' 'Oh, I thought you were much older…' and so on. It's been really stressful, I can tell you that!"

"Well, you can't change anything now. You've become a celebrity in our small town." Kevin rose and went over to her. He stroked Diablo's neck lovingly as the horse ate from the feed trough. "Well, you V.I.P., does it taste good?"

"What do you mean, V.I.P.?"

"Very important pony!"

"Oh, yeah, of course! Well, I think he doesn't even notice all the excitement. He's just happy about all the carrots he's received."

"Hey, what do you two think? Do you want to go riding?" Lillian stretched her back and joined her friends.

"Oh, I don't know." Ricki looked at Kevin, who just waved off her doubts.

"No problem. Go ahead! I'll just stay here and do some work and groom the other horses. By the look of them, they could all use some attention!"

"You could ride Frisbee."

"Oh, no!" Kevin rejected the offer at once. "I'm never going to ride other people's horses again! The last time was enough for me. I don't want anything else to happen."

"Nonsense," said Lillian. "What happened with Holli will never happen again."

"Exactly! And that's why I am staying here." Kevin turned aside to get the grooming equipment.

"Now wait a minute," called Ricki after him. "You know that Mrs. Unger can't ride her Frisbee anymore. She herself offered – no, actually insisted – that we should ride him. After all, what can happen with Frisbee? He's the most gentle horse the riding academy ever had. Anyway, we have to ride slowly so we don't overdo it with Holli."

"Good, than do it! Have fun." Kevin turned his back on them and disappeared for a few minutes.

"Bummer," sighed Ricki. She would have liked to have him along, but she understood his reservation.

"Come on," prodded Lillian. "Just an hour! You can handle one hour without Kevin, can't you?"

Ricki punched her lightly. "Don't tease me! Okay, let's go."

She took Diablo's halter and led him beside her in order to tie him up. While she groomed him, Lillian chased after Holli.

"I can't believe it! Holli, you little beast, stay still."

But the horse was not about to let his owner catch him. This was such a fun game. He kept letting her get within six feet of him, and then he turned and trotted away.

"That's the disadvantage to a box stall," panted Lillian as she ran after him.

Kevin, who had began to brush Sugar in the meantime, laughed out loud. Holli stood still right in front of him and turned his head toward Lillian.

"Hold him still," she yelled, but he had already trotted away.

"Should I saddle Diablo, or are we playing tag with our horses?" Ricki leaned against Diablo's shoulder and watched with interest.

"Our two-legged person is catching up. She goes into

21

the sharp right turn onto the straight lane! She's coming closer and closer to Doc Holliday, who seems to be out of breath. Now, Lillian Bates is neck and neck with the white horse! Ladies and gentlemen, this is the most exciting race since Doc Holliday and Diablo. Attention! They are neck and neck on the homestretch, and it looks as though the two-legged one is going to win. But no, it's unbelievable! Ladies and gentlemen, the white horse is taking the lead and is going to do an extra length...now..." Kevin talked so rapidly that he got red in the face, but Ricki was laughing uncontrollably.

Lillian panted like a locomotive engine and wondered for the hundredth time why the barn on her parents' little farm had to be so large. "That's it – stop – over! I give up!" Gasping for breath, she fell back onto a bale of hay.

Holli whinnied in triumph. *I win,* he seemed to say, and that's the way the three friends saw it too.

"Did you hear that? He's laughing at you," said Kevin, and Ricki joined in the merry teasing: "Are you going to just sit back and take that?"

"I would run too, if you were after me, isn't that so, Holli? We men won't let women catch us!"

"Is that so?" Ricki said, raising her eyebrows.

Holli's owner was bent over, hands on her thighs, still trying to catch her breath. "Women! Don't make me laugh! Why don't *you* catch him instead of bragging," she said between breaths. "I'll bet you can't catch him either."

"Bet I can. What do I get when I do it?"

"Hmm," thought Lillian.

"I know!" Ricki snapped her fingers. "The loser has to invite the winner for ice cream this evening! Me too, of course. After all, I'm your referee."

"Okay." Kevin laughed, sure of himself. "Lily, take your wallet."

"I told you two, never call me Lily! Let's go, hero!"

"Okay, if that's all–Holli, come to me!"

The girls watched closely as Kevin walked toward Holli and suddenly produced a carrot from his pocket. He held the carrot, which was supposed to be for Diablo, out to the horse. Doc Holliday pointed his ears as he heard the boy's voice. He focused on the treat and started walking toward him. It was easy for Kevin to grab his halter while the horse ate the carrot greedily.

"I can't believe it! The man has Holli's favorite treat in his pocket and doesn't say anything! He lets me run around for hours, amusing himself taking advantage of me! Oh, no! Okay, Kevin, you're going to be moved down in the sympathy list!"

"No, not again! Holli, give the carrot back immediately, otherwise your owner might use it against me. So, I'd like a strawberry sundae with whipped cream," the boy said, and Ricki couldn't wait for her triple-chocolate thick shake.

"You two must be dreaming," Lillian shook her head pretending to be upset. "That would take the rest of my pocket money. Anyway, the whole thing was a sham, Madam Referee – any idiot can catch Holli with a carrot."

Kevin couldn't stop grinning.

"You didn't say how Holli was supposed to be caught," responded Ricki.

"It's unfair! And you aren't an impartial judge." Lillian tried to save her pocket money one last time.

"Okay," Kevin took his hand away from the halter for a minute. –"ice cream or Holli?"

"You blackmailer!" groaned Doc Holliday's owner. "Okay, ice cream!"

"Yes! A woman keeps her word!"

Lillian smiled in spite of her defeat. With her breathing back to normal, she took her horse and led him next to Diablo, who was becoming restless and moved one of his legs back and forth.

"All right, let's change the subject," said Holli's owner as she took the brush and currycomb from Ricki's hand.

"If I have to get my own grooming stuff, it'll be too late," she said while she proceeded to give her Hanoverian a quick going-over before saddling him.

"Well, that should do us for a short ride," she said apologetically to Ricki, whose Diablo had been gazing longingly at the door for several minutes now.

Ricki pulled out a lock of Diablo's mane from behind his headband. "We're leaving in a minute, sweetie," she said reassuringly.

Five minutes later, both girls were saddled and leaving the barn, happily chatting together.

Kevin waved after them before turning back to the other horses and beginning the grooming. Lovingly he began to brush Frisbee, but all he could think of was having his own horse. Would this dream ever be fulfilled? Kevin wasn't so sure. With his parents' divorce hearing in a few days, it was doubtful that his mother, with whom he lived, would have enough money afterward to buy him a horse.

He sighed and leaned against Frisbee. "Maybe I should have gone riding after all," he said to himself. Then turning back to the chore at hand, he resumed currying.

# Chapter 2

After Lillian had made good on her bet loss at the ice-cream shop, Kevin accompanied Ricki home.

"Are you going to come in for a while?" asked Ricki, and Kevin nodded enthusiastically. "Gladly! There's probably a fight going on at my house, so I won't miss anything good."

Just as they were coming in, they ran into Jake, who had been called down to dinner by Brigitte.

"Good evening, you two. Everything okay?"

"Hello, Jake. Thanks, we're fine. What are you up to?"

The old man looked sad. "Well, what would I be doing? I just sit around and snore with Lupo. How's Diablo? I haven't seen him for a long time."

Ricki heard longing in his voice, and decided to ask her parents to drive Jake out to the Bates farm in the next few days so that he could visit Diablo. She was sure that after having spent his whole life with horses, Jake must miss being at the stable.

"We went riding today," said Ricki on their way to the kitchen. "Diablo bolted at a deer, but otherwise it was great. I think I'll have to go riding in the woods more often.

Since the fire, he gets spooked easily. Lily has a similar problem with Holli."

"It will take some time before the animals forget that terrible night. Did you ride too, Kevin?"

The boy shook his head. "No, I stayed behind and cleaned up the stable. Frisbee's coat is now shiny and he looks as new as the day he was born."

The old man nodded kindly. "That's necessary too. I'd like nothing better than to go with you to the barn every day," he added a little sadly. But he knew that because of his heart he could no longer do the strenuous work he used to.

Together the three of them entered the large, bright kitchen, where Brigitte had just set the table.

"Hi, Mom," Ricki greeted her mother.

"Good evening, Mrs. Sulai. I'm here again."

"Oh, Kevin, hi... hello, Ricki dear.. I knew I'd need another place setting!" Brigitte laughed, and in that moment, Kevin felt at home. He was happy that Ricki was his girlfriend and that she had such a warm and caring family – unlike his own.

"Can I help you with anything?" he asked politely.

Brigitte gave him the loaf of bread. "If you want to, you could cut the bread."

"I'm glad you don't need me," Ricki grinned.

"Oh, I have something for you to do too, daughter dear. Please go down to the cellar and bring up a few bottles of spring water – and take the empty bottles with you."

"Okay, Mom." Ricki rolled her eyes. If there was anything she hated to do, it was going down to the cellar where she imagined fat black spiders lurked in the corners just waiting for their victims. Ricki had to control herself so that she didn't drop the bottles in panic when she thought she saw one of those monster spiders. She felt so foolish when the spider turned out to be just some dried leaves.

While she was down in the cellar, Harry rushed into the kitchen and bumped into Kevin, who was just about to sit down.

"What are you doing here again?" he asked nastily, rubbing his forehead.

"I just brought Ricki home."

"How come? Did she forget the way?"

"Harry, please!" Brigitte pushed him into his chair.

"Don't you get anything to eat at home?" asked Harry, and Kevin turned a pale shade of red.

"Harry, that's enough! Kevin is our guest and he is always welcome. Be polite, okay."

Ricki's brother mumbled something unintelligible before he said in a somewhat louder voice, "Then I'll bring someone as a guest, too. Ralph, Stevie, Carl, and –"

"But will there still be enough room for me at the table?" Marcus entered the kitchen in a good mood. "Good evening everyone. Where's Ricki?"

"She's catching spiders!" Harry just couldn't keep his mouth shut, especially when it came to making fun of his sister's fears.

"So she's getting water from the cellar. Good, I am really thirsty."

\*

After everyone had eaten dinner and the table had been cleared, Marcus asked them all to stay seated.

Harry began to complain, because he really wanted to

watch television, and Ricki would have preferred to talk with Kevin alone in her room.

"The television isn't going anywhere, and you two can talk later," Ricki's father said. "I wanted to discuss something with you, which is more important than *The Simpsons,*" he added firmly, with a sidelong glance at Harry.

"Uh oh, a family conference! What's up?" Ricki said, a bit bored but sat back down on her chair.

Marcus looked at everyone to make sure they were all listening, then he announced his news.

"So, dear family, your mother and I have been thinking that this house is too small for us all in the long run." Jake was about to protest, but Marcus had anticipated that. "Jake, this doesn't have anything to do with you living here. We've dreamed of moving into a bigger house a little farther out in the country for a long time."

"Wow, that's great! Where?" Ricki was entirely in favor of her father's suggestion, but Harry had tears in his eyes.

"Leave here? I don't want to go. I have my room here, and school, and my friends."

"Take it easy, son. We won't be going far. You'll still go to the same school and have all your old friends. Anyway, we want to hear your opinions first. But what we're thinking of is buying a little farmhouse somewhere. Then we could put up Diablo in our own barn and –"

"Yessss! That would be super! And Jake could see him every day!" Ricki sprang from her seat totally excited, while the old man at the table hid his joy behind the handkerchief he took from his pocket to blow his nose.

Kevin, however, looked cheerless.

"What's wrong, Kevin? Don't you like the idea?" Brigitte asked, laying her hand gently on his arm.

28

"Well, I hope you don't move too far away. I mean, Ricki and I…" He stopped talking.

"I know what you're going to say, and I think I can calm your fears. We like this area very much, and if we look for a new house, it will be nearby."

"Then it's fine," answered Kevin, visibly relieved. "After all, I don't know yet where Mom and I will find a new apartment."

Now Ricki looked glum. "Shoot, I didn't even think of that. When are your parents getting the divorce?"

"Thursday, next week, I think, but we can't move out until later. I hope Mom finds someplace appropriate for us to live soon. I can't stand being with my father any longer."

Brigitte and Marcus glanced at each other with concern. This was the first time they'd heard of Kevin's parents divorcing.

Jake cleared his throat. "Well, if I may say something, I like the idea about the farm, especially because of Diablo, but if it's only about the space, I could move out. After all, Ricki had to give up her room for me, and if I had known that before, I –"

"Stop it! That's total nonsense!" Ricki didn't let Jake finish, and the rest of the family didn't let him get another word in either.

"I won't let you go!" said Harry. "Even if I have to share a room with Ricki for the rest of my life!"

\*

As Ricki and Lillian saddled their horses after school the next afternoon, they didn't need to do too much persuading

29

for Kevin to join them on Frisbee. At first he was a little unsure of himself, because he couldn't get the memory of his accident with Doc Holliday out of his mind, but at the first gallop along a stretch of field path leading to the woods, he laughed openly.

"Man, I really missed that!" he shouted boisterously, and Ricki was happy for him too. If only Kevin had his own horse again.

"What are you two doing on Saturday afternoon?" asked Lillian suddenly.

"No idea, probably riding," answered Ricki, with a shrug, and Kevin agreed. "Riding would be great," he said, and grinned. "Now that I've gotten a taste of it again, I will probably spend every free minute on Frisbee, at least as long as Mrs. Unger has no other plans for him."

"Oh, you crazy horse lovers!" teased Lillian. "Can't you think of something else sometimes?"

"Ha, like you're the one to talk! Holli this, Holli that. But we're the crazy ones! That just isn't true!"

"Okay, I admit it. But I wanted to ask you if you felt like going to the circus with me."

"Circus? Where is there a circus?"

"At the moment, nowhere, but starting tomorrow, there will be one on the grounds of the old brewery. Don't tell me you haven't seen all the posters?"

"Nope!" Kevin shook his head and Lillian laughed.

"Why do I even ask? All you two see is each other."

"True, but apart from that, I hate circuses. When I see how badly they treat the animals – put them in tiny cages and make them do stupid tricks to earn their daily feed – it just makes me furious." For a moment Kevin looked angry, but an instant later his eyes were shining. In high spirits again, he leaned over Frisbee's neck, took the reins, then looked back at the girls.

"How about it? There is no better path to gallop out of the woods!"

"Sure!"

"Anytime!" And within a few seconds all three galloped away as though the devil were chasing them.

"Our horses should feel how good their life is!" shouted Kevin against the wind.

Diablo, Holli, and Frisbee seemed to enjoy this fast pace. They felt the trust of their riders, who held the reins lightly. It was wonderful to gallop through the shadows of the trees while a few rays of late-spring sunshine broke through the branches.

Ricki was tempted to close her eyes so she could be completely at one with the rhythm of the thundering hooves. In moments like this, it was as though her brain shut itself off and she became a part of Diablo, whose joy over his freedom of motion was expressed in longer and longer strides. Exhilarated, he galloped, following the call of the wind, which seemed to whisper: *Diablo, where are you? Come and fly with me in the lightness of the mo-ment...toward freedom.*

"Huh!" Ricki was torn from her daydreaming as Diablo jumped over a log lying across the path. "Phew! That was close!" Carefully she slowed her horse to a more moderate pace. As she brought the panting Diablo to a halt in order to wait for the others, she settled herself into the saddle again and realized that this kind of riding could be very dangerous.

Recalling Kevin's riding accident, when Holli and Diablo had bolted through a meadow and Holli had

31

stepped in a ditch injuring himself badly, she remembered her decision not to run any more races against the wind. She didn't want a repeat of that performance.

"I'm an idiot, Diablo," she said quietly, as she lovingly stroked her darling horse's neck. "But it was really great, wasn't it, boy?"

"Say, did you rub pepper under his tail? He took off like a rocket." Lillian, a little out of breath, asked when she rode up alongside Diablo.

"Man, didn't you see the log?" Kevin asked, joining the other two. "I thought, now she'll learn how to fly."

Ricki laughed. "It wasn't that bad. I know that Diablo is a good springer."

"Diablo is, but you?" countered Lillian.

Ricki made a face. "Is that supposed to be a comment on my riding skills?"

"Never! How could I? I remember a girl who wanted to participate in an E-jump two years ago and who landed on her neck after the second barrier. What was her name?" Lillian smiled, looking over at Kevin.

"Don't you dare say a word!" Ricki warned him, before the three went happily on their way.

As they turned onto the narrow country road, which bordered two small villages, Ricki said suddenly: "Hey, I have an idea. We could look over all the little farms in the area and see if any of them is vacant. My father wants to meet with a realtor in the next few days, but who knows, maybe by then we will have found our new old house."

"What, what, what? Slowly, so I can understand you. Your family wants to move?" Lillian brought Holli to a halt and turned to her friend in total confusion.

"Didn't I tell you yet? Sorry, I've been a little forgetful

32

recently. Yes, Dad said that we're moving to a bigger house, close by but away from town, and then I'll have my own stall for Diablo."

"That's great!" Lillian was very glad for her friend. She was so happy on her parents' farm and couldn't imagine living in town – or anywhere else. "You don't have anything yet?"

"No. I hope we find something soon!"

"I hope so too!" Kevin joined in the conversation. "Lily, isn't your father in a farmers' group?"

"Yeah, why?"

"Well, then he could keep his ears open; if there's a farm for sale nearby, he'll know about it."

"Hey, that's a great idea." Ricki beamed. "Do you think your father would do that for us?"

"Sure, why not? Then the farmers will have a new topic to gossip about."

"And hopefully we'll have a new farmhouse," added Ricki, before the three trotted away. The conversation about the farmers' group made them forget about looking for vacant farmhouses, and they headed back to Lillian's house, which they reached in a half hour, after a few shortcuts.

"Man, this fresh air makes me dog tired," yawned Ricki as she unsaddled her horse. A nap before dinner was looking real good.

\*

The next morning the wagons of the Montollini Circus arrived. Like a covered-wagon camp in the Old West, the trailers and transport cages were parked in a circle on the gravel driveway leading to the former brewery.

33

The drivers of the wagons got out slowly and stretched their tired backs. It had been a long drive and they hoped to be ahead of other any circuses planning to stop in this town.

Sandro looked around and tried to imagine how many performances they could give.

"Well, what do you think?" Rolanda tapped him on the shoulder.

"Hmm, no idea. It depends if there are lots of children here." He pointed to the right, where already six or seven boys and girls had been attracted by the name Montollini Circus written on the wagons in bright red sprawling letters.

"Hey, you there, come here!" shouted Sandro.

The children jumped, startled. They hesitated and looked at each other, but then, when Sandro beckoned invitingly and shouted again: "Come on. I want to give you something as a gift." The children ran toward him.

Sandro waved a few tickets in the air. "Hello, kids. Would you like to see a performance?" he asked in his theatrical Italian accent. "It starts this evening at 7 p.m. You can have these free tickets. All you have to do is tell everyone you know that the famous Montollini Circus is here and we'll stay for three days at least. The performances are at 2 p.m. and 7 p.m. Between performances, children can ride the camel, the donkey, or the horses. It doesn't cost much."

The children were delighted. They thought it was an honor to advertise the circus and were determined to tell all their friends about the performances. Clutching their free tickets proudly in their hands, they ran away happily to spread the news.

"I hate to be dependent upon a bunch of kids," grumbled

Piotr, who had observed the little scene. He didn't like children and he made no bones about it.

"Don't forget that a circus cannot exist without children," Sandro reminded him. "They're our main source of income, because they are the ones who persuade their parents and friends to come to our performances. And anyway, the children of today are the parents of tomorrow. They will pass on the joy of visiting a circus to their children."

"God, do you really believe that?" Piotr shook his head incredulously. "The era of performers who were really something special is over now. It's the time of computers and television. A little circus like ours doesn't have a chance! Only the large ones with really professional acts and artists from all over the world are still attracting crowds. Unlike us, they're never turned down when they ask for permission to perform in cities."

Sandro turned and looked angrily in Piotr's eyes. "If that's the way you feel, then why are you still here?"

"I've been asking myself that for some time," his son-in-law answered, the dissatisfaction and disdain evident in his voice. Then, he turned around toward the car nearest him, kicked its tire, and walked off in a huff toward his trailer.

Sandro took a deep breath just as Rolanda, who had overheard the exchange between her husband and her father, came up behind him and put a calming hand on his shoulder.

"Piotr has a bad temper. He doesn't mean it." She tried to explain, but the circus owner put up his hand to stop any more excuses.

"No, Piotr knows exactly what he's saying and, if I'm honest with myself, he's probably right about most of it. I just didn't want to accept our situation. But you should know that I have often thought about disbanding our circus. So, enough worrying. The animals need fresh water and something to eat. Please, tell the others that we will begin to put up the tents in an hour."

Rolanda nodded. With a quick kiss on the cheek and a last worried glance at her father, she left him. She knew he needed a few minutes alone to gather his strength, which was necessary if he was to keep this circus alive.

*

Saturday morning, the telephone rang fairly early at the Sulai house. As usual, Ricki won the race against her kid brother to grab the receiver.

"Hello, you've reached the answering machine of the Sulai family. Actually, we are still in bed. But today–"

"Knock it off, Ricki. Enough with the phony answering machine. This is important," Lillian interrupted, trying to get a word in.

"Morning, Lillian. How come you're up so early? Did your rooster wake you?"

"Don't be ridiculous! Pay attention and listen carefully. Last evening I told my father about your moving plans, and he came up with this great idea. You know the Millers, who live up the road from us? My father leased their meadows five years ago, since they gave up farming. Dad says they told him they are thinking of selling their farm so they can move in with their daughter who lives closer to town. Now that they are older, it's too hard for them to drive the tractor or take the car to town every week to do the shopping." Lillian, in her excitement, was talking at warp speed, stopped to take a breath, then continued her rush of words.

36

"Dad thinks your parents should just drive there and talk to the Millers right away, before they change their mind."

Ricki was almost dizzy with excitement.

"Oh my gosh, Lillian, if that works out that would be fabulous! Just imagine, living so close together!"

"Yeah, that would be great, but first it has to happen. Let's not jump the gun and then be disappointed later if the Millers decide against it."

Ricki sighed. "Of course, you're right. So, first thanks a lot. I'm going to get my parents up and tell them. I'll drop by later. Do you want to go riding?"

"Sure. Is Kevin coming too?"

"I don't know. I'll call him later. See you."

"So long."

Ricki slammed down the receiver and started in the direction of her parents' bedroom.

"What's going on?" asked Harry, rubbing the sleep from his eyes. "Where's the fire?"

"Don't make stupid jokes!" Ricki glared at her brother accusingly. "I've had enough fires for the rest of my life!" she said, before knocking softly on her parents' door.

*

Ricki, Kevin, and Lillian had finished brushing all the horses, and now the three friends sat on two big bales of hay, which they had pulled out in front of the barn door into the warm rays of the spring sun.

Ricki swung her feet back and forth excitedly. She just couldn't sit still.

While Harry was at home with Jake, playing checkers, and listening to his latest ghost stories, her parents were sitting in the Millers' cozy living room talking about the house.

"I wish I were a mouse and could listen in on what they are saying," said Ricki for the umpteenth time.

"Gee, you are so annoying today! You'll know in about an hour at the latest and, as far as mice go, do you have any idea how many cats the Millers have? An animal shelter is nothing in comparison."

"Do they all belong on the farm?" asked Kevin, and Lillian laughed.

"Oh, no, none of them. Cats come and go on a farm. Most of them are strays and just eat before moving on. Say, didn't we want to go riding?"

"As far as I'm concerned, I'm ready to roll," grinned Kevin, standing to stretch.

But Ricki just rolled her eyes. "We can ride later. I just can't leave before I know if buying the Millers' house worked out. After all, it's about Diablo's new home!"

*

Lillian and Kevin exchanged knowing smiles. In a way, they could understand Ricki's impatience. They would probably feel the same if their roles were reversed.

"Do you think ice cream would help nervous farm ailments," Lillian asked her friend.

"For sure!" Ricki brightened. "Did you lose another bet that I don't know about or did you get a raise in your allowance?" Kevin joked.

"Neither," answered Lillian happily. "My mother thought of three suffering young people yesterday while she was shopping."

"Well, if that's the case, let's go!"

38

"I knew it." Dave Bates filled his pipe and sat back in his porch chair with satisfaction. Ricki's father had just thanked him for the good tip about the Millers.

As Margaret Bates passed around glasses of ice-cold lemonade, Marcus told about meeting the Millers.

The elderly couple was skeptical at first, as Brigitte and Marcus stood in their doorway asking them about the house. But when they heard that Dave Bates had sent them, they became more approachable, and invited them in to talk over freshly baked banana muffins and coffee.

Of course they hadn't thought that a buyer for their house would appear so quickly, particularly since they hadn't definitely made up their minds to sell. They hadn't even spoken to a real estate agent and had no idea what their house and property were currently worth.

But they liked the Sulais and had a feeling that Marcus and Brigitte would love their farm as much as they do, so they took them on a tour of the house, the stalls, and through the little cottage that stood across from the main house.

"When we were still farming on a large scale, we had our harvest help live there each year," Hubert Miller explained as they entered the main room of the small house. "Over time though, it began to look a little dilapidated, but the foundations are solid."

Brigitte heard the melancholy in his voice, as if he wished he could turn back time. In spite of the hard work, she thought the Millers must have had a happy life here.

"Finally Mr. Miller asked us very cautiously, if we thought $190,000 would be too much," said Marcus, continuing his account of the meeting with a merry wink at his wife, who could not hide her happiness.

39

"And? I mean, $190,000 sounds like a lot of money...what did you say?" Ricki asked impatiently.

"Well, it is a lot of money, but not for this property. After all, there's the land – the meadows will remain his – two houses, the barn, and stalls. So we agreed. Next week, we'll go to the bank and sign the papers, and we can move in about four weeks. The Millers' daughter is coming next week to help them pack. Since their move to her house was planned anyway, it'll be sooner rather than later." Marcus paused and then said: "We'll renovate our new home little by little, as we have the time." He looked at his daughter, who started to cry with happiness.

"Oh, happy day!" she began to sing, completely off key, hugging Kevin and Lillian as she danced around them like a crazy woman.

Lillian grabbed her by the shoulders and shook her. "You ride better than you sing."

Ricki ran to the door. "Exactly, so what are we waiting for? Let's ride over to the Millers' farm so Diablo can see where he's going to live." And with that she skipped down the porch steps and ran to the barn.

"As if Ricki has never rode by that house before!" Lillian couldn't help laughing.

"See you later," shouted Kevin and Lillian to the adults, before they ran after their friend.

"Nutty kids," mumbled Marcus, but he and Brigitte were just as happy as their daughter was. They still didn't know what Harry and Jake would think of the news, but they were sure that they would be happy too.

# Chapter 3

About a half-hour earlier, the three friends had ridden past Ricki's future home. It looked old but very romantic, with a huge pear tree climbing up a trellis on the south side to the gable and reaching upward with its broad branches.

"Oh, what a beautiful morning–oh, what a beautiful day…" sang Ricki, still totally over the moon with joy.

Lillian winced at her friend's off-key vocalizing, but decided not to kid her about it – this time. "I think you're in a time warp. It's already noon. Morning is long gone."

"Oh, I keep thinking how fantastic it will be when Diablo is in his own stall. You're happy about that too, aren't you, sweetie?" Ricki nuzzled her horse's neck. She slid back and forth on her saddle with excitement, and that bothered Diablo. Shaking his head in disapproval, he sprang suddenly to one side.

"Whoa, what's that all about? Stop fooling around!"

"Your devil is just echoing your excitement!" laughed Lillian. "If you were a little less wound up, we could enjoy this wonderful, peaceful ride. I think this is one of life's best moments…the sound of horses' hooves, their neighing, feeling their swaying gait, the sunshine, fresh air and, apart from the singing of birds, just divine quiet. It's times like this I realize just how wonderful life is."

At that very second a motorcycle rider drove past and revved up his engine, just as he came parallel with the horses.

"Well, that's the end of the romantic interlude!" Furious, Kevin looked in the direction of the driver. "What a stupid idiot! We're really lucky that our horses are used to traffic or someone could have really gotten hurt."

"They should take away his driver's license," replied Ricki angrily. Only Lillian remained calm.

"Oh, you guys, don't get upset. There are always losers like that around who love to show off. Look up there," she pointed to the top of the hill at the old brewery. "The circus wagons are already there. Come on, let's ride over there and see if it's worth going to one of the performances."

"Do we have to?" grumbled Kevin, but when Ricki happily agreed with Lillian's suggestion, he gave in.

The closer they came to the wagons, the more nervous their horses became. Holli stretched his head up high, puffed out his nostrils, and inhaled the scent of the unknown animals. Frisbee, who had never been nervous before, started to dance back and forth, and Kevin had to work hard to keep him in line. Diablo's ears were in constant motion until he stopped suddenly and gave a loud, almost challenging, whinny.

"It's okay, sweetie, this isn't anything special," Ricki said soothingly, trying to calm down her horse. But Diablo obviously didn't agree with her.

Ricki gave a slight nudge with her thigh to move him along, but Diablo reared up almost vertically into the air, his rider just managing to hang on by instinctively bending

42

forward and holding onto his neck. That way Ricki changed the weight distribution, so that her horse didn't fall over backward.

"Diablo, stop!" she screamed at her horse, but he was acting almost crazy. "My God, what's wrong with you?"

Ricki hardly had time to catch her breath, when her horse reared up again.

Lillian had turned pale and had her own problems trying to control. But Kevin reacted quickly, moving Frisbee beside Diablo, and before Ricki's horse could rear up a third time, he grabbed Diablo's reins and forced him to stay on the ground. He spoke to him calmly as he glanced sideways at Ricki, who was gray in the face and shaking in the saddle.

"Are you okay?" he asked after Diablo had become a little quieter. The horse's eyes were still glassy with fear, and he was staring at the men who had interrupted their work with the circus animals to watch the drama he had caused in front of the wagons.

"Yes. Now. Thanks, Kev." Ricki was puzzled by Diablo's reaction. "I wonder what could have set him off like that." Her friends had no idea either.

Rolanda was just leading Sharazan out of the stable tent so that she could brush him in the sunlight. But the tall roan sensed the strange horses and started to whinny excitedly.

The young woman had difficulty tying him to the lead rope. "Hey, my baby, behave! They won't hurt you! They'll be glad if you don't hurt them."

Ricki, Lillian, and Kevin decided to turn around and ride back. They didn't want to risk anything happening to themselves or their horses. As they rode away, Kevin turned to look back once more. Just for a moment, he glanced at Sharazan, whose coat shone in the sunshine like a golden tapestry. He thought his heart would stand still. That animal looked like the reincarnation of his Leonardo, only bigger and much thinner.

The youth swallowed hard. His dream horse was standing back there, and he couldn't get any closer to him because Diablo would bolt if he tried.

"That just can't be true," he mumbled to himself, completely overcome by the beauty of the circus horse.

And, as he turned around for a last look, he saw a girl standing beside the wonderful creature. He strained his eyes for a better look, but the riders were already too far away for him to be sure who that person was. But he was almost positive it was Cathy, who had stood there unmoving, staring after them.

*

Frightened, Cathy had watched Diablo's behavior from the stable tent and worried that her former friend, Ricki, could be catapulted out of the saddle at any minute.

*Thank God Kevin intervened,* she thought, and was relieved to see that the riders had turned back.

She looked at them riding away with longing. She would have loved to be with them, like before, but she knew it was her own fault that nothing was the same as it had been half a year ago.

She had argued with herself so often and asked herself a thousand times why she had allowed Lark to have so much influence over her. That girl had really ruined her life.

"No, I ruined it myself!" she admitted bitterly.

Lark had written her a letter from her new home and

hadn't once mentioned anything about what had happened. No apologies, no "I'm sorry." There was nothing in her letter that would have made Cathy want to answer her. And so she ended this unusual, burdensome friendship.

"Girl, are you dreaming? I thought you wanted to help me groom the horses." Rolanda poked Cathy a little harshly in her side with the currycomb. "Helping means helping and not standing around," she said. "Otherwise, no free ticket," she added.

"Yeah, okay," answered Cathy almost tonelessly, before turning to Rashid, the dun-colored horse Rolanda had also tied up outside the tent.

Cathy had ridden her bike to the old brewery that morning, like she did every other time she heard that a circus had come to town. She loved the atmosphere of the circus, being around the performers and working with the animals. She always helped out when a circus was in town and got a free ticket in return.

Today was the first time, however, that she had been there alone. Before, Ricki had always been with her, and together they had had lots of fun with the circus folk.

*

"Did you see that black horse?" Piotr was walking by with Juan, the big-cat tamer, who was the only circus performer who used his real name, and Cathy had heard part of their conversation.

"He's really powerful, isn't he? If he were in the ring and your panther sprang through a flaming hoop on his back…"

Juan smiled broadly, so that his white teeth gleamed.

45

"Yeah, wouldn't that be something! If only we had a lot of money and could buy that devil."

"Stop talking about money!" Piotr's face changed immediately. "When I think about it, I could just... This afternoon, I have to go begging. We'll see if the local farmers have enough hay and straw to give us some for free. I hate to be humiliated like this."

Cathy couldn't hear what Juan said to that. In any case, for whatever reason, she had disliked Piotr from the first moment she saw him.

He looks cunning, somehow, she thought, and she promised herself to stay away from him. She could sense that the man was trouble.

After she had brushed Rashid, she stepped back and admired her work. The horse was almost as beautiful as Sharazan, who was already finished.

Cathy looked around quickly, and when she didn't see Rolanda anywhere, she took out some sugar cubes and fed them to the horses.

"Rolanda would be furious if she saw that. So chew a little faster," she begged the horses, and then she leaned against Rashid's neck dreamily.

The dun turned his head to Cathy and let it sink heavily onto her shoulder. It was love at first sight between Cathy and the lovely animal, and it had started that morning as Cathy stood opposite him and became aware how thin both of the horses were.

*That's terrible,* she thought, and decided to ask Rolanda why.

*

Ricki, Kevin, and Lillian had ridden straight back to the Bates farm. Their fright over Diablo's behavior was still fresh in their minds.

"He acted like a wild horse," Ricki told Jake when she was back home sitting with him and discussing Diablo's scary antics of earlier that day. "Mom would have had a fit if she had seen today's ride."

"Hmmm..." Jake stroked Lupo's back as he gazed off thoughtfully, trying hard to remember something.

"If only my brain weren't so rusty. There was some-thing, something with a circus. Wait, give a minute to think of it . . . "

He didn't say anything for a while, just shook his head angrily from time to time.

Ricki observed him closely, and every now and then she stole a look at her watch. The waiting seemed endless to her, but the hands on her watch hardly moved.

It had been about five minutes when Jake's face sudden-ly lit up.

"Exactly! That's exactly the way it was! Now I remem-ber. Do you remember me telling you about the Summersfield horse ranch, where Diablo was born?"

Jake looked at Ricki and waited for an answer. When she nodded, he continued.

"Well, at the time, when I was working for them and Diablo was still a foal, there was a circus in town, and they had pitched their tents on the meadow of our ranch. They were there for a week, and lots of people came to the per-formances. At that time we had a so-called stable boy who worked only a few hours a week. I never liked him. You can't imagine! He was dissatisfied with everything and al-ways in a bad mood. No one ever did anything right by

47

him, he hated his job, and he often took out his frustration on the animals, especially the trusting foals. If anything had made him mad, he sometimes hit them over the head with the broom, and if they didn't get out of the way fast enough when he was cleaning out the stalls, he would poke them in the pastern with the manure fork. Diablo was one of the victims of his anger."

Ricki shook her head in disbelief. "And they let such a man work on a horse ranch?"

"Well," Jake shook his head slowly back and forth, remembering. "You can imagine that once I saw this, I wouldn't put up with it, and he was warned; then, after two months, he was fired. Right after that he went to work for the circus, and helped put up and take down the tents and was the general handyman. I don't know if he was happy there. I think someone told me he married the daughter of the circus owner, but I don't know if it was true. No idea."

Jake paused for a minute, and Ricki wondered what all this had to do with Diablo's behavior.

"That wicked little gnome – I think his name was Henley or Hinkle or something like that – after he was hired by the circus, he came over to the bordering paddock the day the circus was to leave. I was just brushing Diablo as he came up and stared at Diablo with a mean glint in his eye. 'Because of you stupid animals, I lost my job,' he said, and before I could prevent him, he kicked Diablo hard against the front leg. My God, how he laughed when he heard the foal cry out in pain. I would have liked to beat him up, you can believe me, but Diablo was more important, and so I led him away, limping. I will never forget that horrible laugh and Diablo won't either. When Henley – or whatever his name was – turned his back on us and started

48

to leave the paddock, Diablo whinnied really shrilly and started after him. Before Henley reached the fence, the foal had caught up to him and kicked out at him again and again. Diablo hit him a few times, pretty hard actually, and the guy was very glad when he finally got out of his range. The little fella had really given it to him, and he stood at the fence for a long time with his ears laid back and his teeth showing, until all of the circus wagons had left the meadow."

Ricki began to understand. "And you think he was reminded of this guy when he saw the circus wagons?"

Jake shrugged his shoulders. "Maybe. It's possible. I know that Diablo has a very good memory. And he wouldn't have put you in danger without a reason."

*

The girls decided to go to the performance that same evening.

"How come you changed your mind and decided to go with us to the circus?" Lillian asked Kevin, surprised to see him, as he pulled his bike up next to Ricki, who was waiting at the foot of the Bates' porch for Lillian to mount hers.

"Well, somebody has to take care of you girls," he winked. Of course, he didn't want to tell them the real reason yet, but since their last ride together he couldn't think of anything else but the shiny roan that had stood outside the stable tent.

The girls rolled their eyes.

"That's all we need." Ricki gave her boyfriend a kiss on his cheek and a big smile. "Well, I'm glad you're coming with us."

49

She got back on her bike. "We'll have to hurry a little if we want to get there on time," she said after a glance at her watch.

"Okay, let's go!" replied Lillian, and the three friends pedaled away as hard as they could. "By the way, this afternoon there was someone from the circus at our farm. He said they needed feed donations because fewer and fewer people are coming to the performances and they're finding it hard to afford to pay for all the feed they need."

"And did he have any luck with your father?" Kevin wanted to know.

Lillian nodded, breathing heavily from the exertion of pedaling. "Of course, my parents are always open to this kind of need. It's not the animals' fault. Dad promised him a few bales of hay and straw, which he delivered to the brewery right after we had lunch.

"I think that's cool of your father."

Lillian slowed her pedaling to catch her breath, and the others followed.

"But, you know, that guy sort of freaked me out. There was something about him that made my skin crawl!"

"You're starting to act like Diablo!" Ricki said, then told them Jake's story.

"That's very possible," said Kevin, when Ricki was through. "Leonardo had a wonderful memory as well. Even after years, he could still remember who had given him a treat and he would always search their pockets for sugar cubes. Why shouldn't Diablo associate the circus wagons with pain? After all, he saw the man who hit him leave with the wagons."

Ricki and Lillian were convinced as well. But as they approached the circus grounds, the three decided to forget

50

about the episode with Diablo and to focus on the performance. They got off their bikes and leaned them against the fence around the trailers and then they ran over to the ticket booth, where a few people were standing in line. They couldn't wait to see what the little circus had to offer.

While they were looking for their seats in the third row, a pair of eyes peered out between the curtains behind the circus ring.

Cathy quivered as she heard Ricki's laugh. She was fooling around with Kevin and Lillian. Once again Cathy wished she could be friends with them again.

She was pushed aside by Sandro.

"Sit down over there," he said, and pointed to a seat on the edge of the ring. She sat down timidly and hoped that her former friends wouldn't see her. However, since there weren't many people in the audience, she and Ricki soon exchanged glances, and suddenly Ricki didn't feel as happy as she had just minutes before.

"Cathy's sitting over there!" she whispered to Kevin and Lillian. Then she remembered Jake's words: "She was your friend and she will remain your friend. Could you forgive her?" And Ricki felt a twinge of guilt toward her former friend.

"I don't know," she thought out loud, but neither Kevin nor Lillian heard her. The band had started playing the opening music for the performance and Sandro Piccore entered the ring, smiling broadly.

"Good evening, ladies and gentlemen!"

Somewhat bored, the three followed the mediocre program being performed.

"At least the price of admission is for a good cause. I paid the few dollars gladly so that the animals can be taken

51

care of," Ricki whispered to Kevin, while a clown tried to get the meager audience to laugh.

Kevin felt really uncomfortable. A lot of acts were already finished, and the performance was almost over, and still he hadn't seen the roan. He was becoming more and more disappointed. Had he come for nothing?

Sandro had just chased the clown out of the ring. He took off his top hat theatrically and held out his arms, as though he could embrace the whole world.

"Well, dear audience, our performance is almost at an end. But the greatest attraction is still to come. This is the climax of our program! Watch the unforgettable Rolanda, with her two wonderful, unique horses, Sharazan and Rashid, who have mastered the most difficult equestrian drill. Here she is: Rrro-lann-daaa!"

The audience hardly bothered to applaud. They had been too disappointed by the other acts. Only a few small children – and Kevin – were full of anticipation at the mention of the horses.

When the curtains parted, and Sharazan and Rashid galloped around the ring next to each other in fascinating grace and harmony, Kevin's heart almost stopped. Enchanted, he watched every step Sharazan took. He wondered why the circus people had hung such long saddlecloths over the shiny coats of the animals. The movement of the horses would have been even more impressive without the long blankets.

Filled with pride and longing, Cathy stared at Rashid from the other side of the ring. She had brushed and combed him for almost an hour, and his floor-length tail and extraordinarily long mane swayed like a field of wheat in the wind as he galloped.

The teenager couldn't bear to think that the circus would be taking down its tents the day after tomorrow and leaving for an unknown destination. She would miss Rashid more than anything in the world – well, except perhaps her friendship with Ricki, but that was something different.

Sharazan mesmerized Kevin. His girlfriend has been tugging at his sleeve for two minutes, but he seemed not to notice. One thought had become rooted in him:

*Sharazan is the one to come after Leonardo. I'll just have to work on Mom. . .*

When the show ended, Kevin tried to get into the stable tent, while Ricki and Lillian, shaking their heads with displeasure, watched one of the circus people help two very plump children onto the back of a small, spindly donkey.

Chico spread out his legs so he wouldn't lose his balance, and the girls thought the animal would collapse any minute.

"Those kids are much too heavy for that little animal! Don't they see that?" Ricki exploded with indignation, and Lillian agreed: "Maybe the donkey should get his strength back first. He looks as though he hasn't eaten for weeks!"

Overhearing this, the people nearby began to take notice, and some of them turned in anger and left the circus grounds. One child sobbed, "I wanted to ride too," but the mother explained that she didn't want to support people who didn't take care of their animals properly.

The man who was leading Chico around glared at Ricki and Lillian with hatred.

"Whoa, he really looks mean," said Ricki, and Lillian grew pale with fear.

"That's the one I was telling you about," she whispered

53

hoarsely, and she felt the same uneasiness about the man that she had felt in the afternoon, when she saw him at the farm.

Then Piotr came up to the girls with the donkey in tow, a menacing sneer on his face. "Just as I thought!" he hissed. "Don't think you can mess up my business just because your old man gave us a few bales of hay and straw. Get out of here, right now, or do I have to make you?"

He started threateningly toward Lillian, who backed away, scared. The man really looked dangerous.

With a final sad look at the donkey, Ricki and Lillian turned and slowly walked away. The two chubby children were giggling with glee as they kept jabbing their heels into the sides of the animal.

"Yeah, that's right! Prod him along, the old lazybones, so that he gets going!" The ugly voice broke out in a nasty laugh that sounded like the bleating of a goat.

Disgusted, Ricki turned around with an appropriate reply on the tip of her tongue, but Lillian pulled her away.

"Remember Cooper," she pleaded. She didn't want Ricki to be the victim of another violent man. "Let's see if we can find Kevin. I just want to go home."

Ricki nodded. She didn't feel like watching the animals anymore either.

"What we saw was enough. If all the animals are as undernourished, these people deserve to be punished."

"Well, the ones in the performance looked okay."

"That's what you think!" Kevin had just appeared, coming around the corner of a trailer, heading for their bikes, when he heard Lillian's last sentence. His face was bright red with rage.

"I saw the two horses without the blankets! Man, you

54

have no idea how thin they are. You could count every rib. The SPCA should go after them!"

"I think I'm going to be sick," said Ricki, as she tried to check her anger. If there was anything she couldn't stand, it was people who didn't take proper care of their animals.

"I wish I had a huge farm with lots of space, so I could take in all of these animals that aren't being cared for," she said. As she said it, she made up her mind that when she grew up she would find a job helping abused animals.

"Maybe I'll become a vet," she mumbled to herself, but Kevin wasn't listening to her. He got an idea as Ricki was talking about getting a large farm.

"Your parents are buying a house with stalls right now. Do you think you could talk your father into buying some of these animals from the circus and granting them asylum?"

"That's a terrific idea, but I think Dad would kill me if I made that kind of suggestion. We don't have a lot of money, and the house costs will be expensive."

"And you, Lillian? What about you?" Kevin broke in. "Your father can't stand to see animals suffer."

"That's true, but first of all, our barn is full with the horses from the riding academy, and secondly, we're not rich either, but when I think of that little donkey…"

"I'm thinking of Sharazan!" exploded Kevin, and punched his handlebars so hard that Ricki jumped. She had never seen him this angry. But when she looked into his eyes, she understood everything.

"He's the one, isn't he?" she asked quietly, and Kevin nodded seriously.

Lillian looked from one to the other. "Who is what?"

"Sharazan, the roan. He's the one. He's Kevin's new horse!"

55

"Ah. Does Sharazan know yet?"

Kevin didn't answer. Instead, he turned and hopped on his bike and, without saying another word, pedaled away furiously. He knew he had to talk with his mother about it this very evening, although he knew it was the worst possible time for this conversation. After all, his mother had enough problems with the divorce and worrying where they would live without thinking about buying a new horse for her son.

Kevin sighed. And who said that the circus people would be willing to sell Sharazan anyway?

*

That evening all three friends tried to persuade their parents to buy some of the animals from the circus.

Lillian worked on her parents to at least save Chico, the little donkey, to spare him any further suffering. But Dave Bates, while empathizing with his daughter's distress at the mistreatment of the animal, patiently tried to explain his position.

"Even if I wanted to, honey, at the moment I couldn't buy that animal. You know yourself that we don't have any room now. The horses in the barn –"

"But Dad, it's only a matter of time until they're placed somewhere else. And Chico, he doesn't need much space," Lillian pleaded.

"Lillian, please try to understand, we can't help every animal. We can help some by giving them feed to relieve the worst cases, but we can't start buying all the suffering animals, you have to understand that! I'm not a millionaire, you know."

56

Lillian sensed that she was not going to get anywhere with her father right then, but she knew him well enough to be sure that the next day he would drive over to the circus to see for himself if Chico was really suffering.

*Little donkey,* Lillian said silently, *please forgive me, but I hope that horrid man is as mean to you tomorrow as he was today. If he is, you can be sure my dad will take you home that very day!*

Lillian got up from the couch in temporary defeat and left the Bates' living room. Throwing on a sweater, she went to look after the horses before going to bed.

In the stall she hugged her beloved Doc Holliday around the neck while Diablo nudged her behind the knees. Lillian laughed quietly.

"Oh, you two sweetie pies. I hope you know how good you have it."

The horses watched her with huge, understanding eyes as she said good night and quietly left the barn.

*

When Kevin returned home, he heard his parents fighting even before he opened the door. The same money arguments about alimony and child support.

"Don't think you're going to get a cent more than I have to pay you! And as for your son, there are guidelines, thank God!"

Wendell Thomas' voice was filled with rage, while his wife's sounded calculated and harsh.

"If you think I don't know what we are entitled to, then you're wrong!" she replied, her eyes like slits.

Before his father could shout his response, Kevin entered the room. He felt sick, and a mixed feeling of hate and fear lay heavy on his heart. He stared from one parent to the other with fiery cheeks before he exploded: "Can't you stop this? I can't stand it anymore – your endless fighting."

"Aw, the kid can't stand it anymore," Mr. Thomas taunted the youth. Then he stormed out of the room, grabbed his coat from the closet, and banged the door shut after him.

Caroline Thomas let herself fall back into one of the heavy leather armchairs.

"I'll be glad when this is finally over," she sighed. After an embarrassing few moments of silence passed, she faced her son with a tired smile. "Well, dear, how was your day?"

Kevin sat down as well and began to talk.

"...and just imagine, the horses at the circus are so thin that you could count their ribs. And I thought...if we couldn't maybe...Sharazan...buy him..."

Since all his mother did was wrinkle her forehead, Kevin began to fantasize aloud about his dream horse.

"You know, he looks almost like Leonardo, only he is even more golden and his mane is even longer. Mom, I think Sharazan is the only horse I could love as much as Leonardo."

Caroline Thomas seemed to look right through her son. Scenes of the past replayed themselves. She saw Kevin with his beloved gelding on the riding ring in front of their house or in the stable crouched on blankets as Leonardo suffered with colic. She felt Kevin's joy when he returned from riding with shiny eyes, and also Kevin's pain as his father literally trained the horse to death. She had felt guilty about it all these years and she had known, although Kevin never spoke about it, that no other horse could take

58

Leonardo's place in his heart. She was all the more surprised that her son had begun to talk about it himself.

Kevin's mother went over her finances in her head. She knew that she would have to watch her expenses carefully in the future. After all, she would have to furnish a new apartment, pay rent, and manage the other household expenses from her alimony payments until she found a job. But when she looked into Kevin's shining, hopeful eyes, she knew that somehow everything would work out if only he were happy again – like he was with Leonardo.

"I think I owe you," she whispered softly. "Let's try to buy this animal. But I have to tell you in advance that I can't spend more than twenty-five hundred dollars, otherwise we'll be in deep financial trouble."

Kevin caught his breath. "Does that mean, does that mean that Sharazan? I mean…"

Caroline nodded slowly and swallowed a few tears as her son jumped out of his chair with a shout of joy, hugged her, and planted a big thank-you kiss on her cheek.

*My God, how long had it been since the boy had been so happy?* Caroline thought as she saw her son's demeanor change before her eyes. As for Kevin, he was the happiest person in the world, it seemed to him, even though his parents were getting divorced.

\*

Ricki sat moodily at the kitchen table, her teeth clenched and her face a bright red. Her eyes sparkled angrily, and she was so upset that she couldn't eat a thing, although her empty stomach was growling.

"What's up? What's put you in such a bad mood? Was

the performance that bad?" Brigitte tried to get her daughter to smile, but Ricki just snorted.

"The performance after the performance was terrible…a gigantic mess!"

She just couldn't hold back any longer and began to tell the story.

Marcus listened attentively to his daughter. He was thankful to Lillian that she had held Ricki back, although he could understand completely why his daughter was so upset. But when she begged him to save one of the circus animals, he shook his head emphatically.

"No, Ricki, that would be going too far."

"But why? We would have enough space on the new farm."

"That may be, but every animal costs money to buy and to maintain. And considering that you have Diablo now, I think you'll understand that as much as I feel sorry for the animals, I can't do this favor for you right now. After all, the farm has to be renovated, the stalls have to be rebuilt, and the lawyer will cost money. No, we simply cannot afford any extra expenses."

Ricki was overtired and close to tears.

"Mom, why don't you say something?"

Brigitte put a comforting arm around Ricki's shoulders. "Your father's right. At the moment we can't spend any more money."

"Jake?" Ricki looked to her old friend for help, but he shook his head as well.

"You know very well that isn't possible. Try to understand that you can't help every animal in need. But you did help Diablo, so always remember that you can be proud of yourself for giving at least one animal a good life."

Ricki mumbled something incomprehensible and then got up abruptly.

"I'm going to bed. Good night, everyone!"

Brigitte glanced at Ricki's plate, where her sandwich lay still uneaten. "Don't you want to eat something?" But the girl was on her way upstairs and didn't hear her mother's question. She closed the door to the bathroom a little more loudly than usual just as Jake was saying, "By morning she will have calmed down." Once inside, she leaned on the sink and stared at herself in the mirror.

"Are you proud of yourself?" she asked her reflection, which slowly shook its head in response.

"See! Proud, what nonsense! I'm happy for Diablo, but proud? What a horrible word."

With this recognition, she hastily washed her face and hurried into the bedroom she shared with Harry, who was already snoring softly. She was so glad that tomorrow was Sunday, and she could sleep in.

# Chapter 4

"Ann, I have to talk to you!"

Rolanda was noticeably startled. When Sandro called her by her real name, it usually meant the start of a very serious conversation.

"Can't we talk later? I want to take care of the horses."

"No!" Sandro's voice sounded harsher than he had intended. "Come in and close the door!"

It was oppressively hot inside the owner's trailer, although it was only 11 a.m. and summer was still a few weeks away.

"Is the air conditioner broken again?" asked Rolanda. Sandro glanced at her with annoyance.

"You could have spared us that question! You know we haven't had enough money all year to have it fixed!"

Rolanda sat down at the little table and observed her father with mixed feelings as he silently paced back and forth in the tight space. She knew something was bothering him, but she didn't dare speak because she knew it was something bad.

\*

Lillian's parents were on their way back from church.

"Let's drive past the old brewery. I want to see if Fred has already rotated his bordering meadow. If he has, I could borrow the roller tomorrow and start in with our –"

Margaret Bates tried to suppress a smile, but it didn't work. "Why don't you just say that you can't get that poor donkey Lillian was talking about out of your mind?"

"Nonsense, I need the roller, that's all," her husband, Dave, answered a little too quickly.

"Well, I think donkeys are cute," continued Margaret, coyly leading her husband along. "And normally, they aren't expensive. Darling, you aren't going to give me a donkey for our anniversary, are you?" she asked naively.

Dave braked hard because he had almost missed the turn off to the brewery.

"Well," he gave in, "not exactly for our anniversary, but if you think they're cute, we could consider getting one anyway. What do you think?"

He pulled up in front of the circus ticket booth and looked tenderly at his wife. So she had known all along, just like Lillian, what would happen.

*I love this man,* Margaret Bates thought happily, as they walked toward the stable tent together. She had put three very large carrots and a few sugar cubes in her handbag before they drove to church.

Margaret knew that soon she would be driving home alone and that her Dave would be walking the two and a half miles home in his best clothes, dragging a donkey, provided what he saw today confirmed what Lillian had said.

*

63

Cathy rode her bike around the corner of the main entrance to the circus tent and leaned it against the first trailer. She was happy that she could spend another day with her Rashid, as she'd come to think of him, before the circus left town tomorrow. She was just about to enter the stable tent when she heard the angry voice of Lillian's father.

"That is unbelievable. I've seen a lot of animals in bad condition, but never as bad as this little donkey. He's just skin and bones...and his hooves, they're starting to grow upward! What a mess! They should shut you down and take away all your animals! Where's your boss? Call him, I want to speak to him immediately!"

Piotr smiled contemptuously, which made him look like an evil villain.

"Oh, look, it's the nice patron from next door!" he said with as much sarcasm as he could muster. "Thanks again for the hay and now, get out of here! Leave!"

"I'll be darned if I will!" thundered Dave Bates, while his wife went over to the donkey, who was pressing against the wall of the tent in fear, fright glazing his eyes.

"Margaret, untie him and take him outside!"

"But I can't just –"

"Do what I say! Untie him!"

Dave Bates stared at Piotr, who was slowly reaching for the long whip that was lying on the ground.

"Just wait, farmer! I'll show you. You won't steal any of the animals!"

"I don't intend to! Don't worry, I want to buy the donkey."

Piotr's mean grin grew broader.

"Buy? Anyone can say that! Get out, right now!" He brandished the whip threateningly.

64

"Where's your boss?" asked Lillian's father again, and slowly removed his Sunday jacket. The expression on Piotr's face became even harder.

"Oh, man, this is not going to end well," Cathy said. She had been standing dead still in the entrance to the tent, listening to the altercation. Now she moved toward past Mrs. Bates, who had become pale with worry.

"I'll get Sandro!" Cathy said to her and ran from the tent. Lillian's mother didn't know who Sandro was, but was relieved to know that someone was coming to separate the two men.

Cathy pounded on the door of Sandro's trailer. "Sandro! Rolanda! Open up – quick!"

Angrily, the circus owner opened the door.

"What the devil –"

"Quick...Piotr...in the stable tent..." stammered Cathy, unable to catch her breath. "Quick, otherwise something awful is going to happen!"

Sandro didn't wait to get the whole story, but he knew something was very wrong. He charged out of the trailer and ran in the direction of the stable tent. He got there just in time to grab the whip out of Piotr's hand before he could strike Dave Bates with it again.

Lillian's father was on the ground holding his bleeding arm.

"Darn it, Piotr, are you crazy? What are you doing?" Sandro pushed his son-in-law away. Piotr's eyes gleamed insanely.

"He wanted to steal Chico! I caught him just in time, as he was untying him."

"What?" Confused, Sandro stared at Lillian's father, waiting for an explanation.

"That's not true!" Cathy, who had followed Sandro into the tent, went to stand beside Mr. Bates. "This is the father of my friend, and he wanted to speak with you, Sandro, because he wants to buy Chico, but Piotr wanted to throw him out."

The owner still didn't understand what had happened between the two men. He asked Dave Bates to accompany him to his trailer so that his arm could be taken care of, and shot Piotr a look of anger that was unmistakable. He knew that the actions of his son-in-law would have unfortunate consequences for the circus.

*

"And then? What happened then?" Ricki was listening to Lillian's story with tears in her eyes while she lovingly stroked the donkey between his ears.

"Well," Lillian continued, "the circus owner offered my father Chico if he didn't report the incident with that horrible Piotr to the police. He wanted to sell everything anyway, he said. Apparently they are so broke that they couldn't be any broker!"

Ricki chuckled. "'Broker,' what kind of word is that?

Lillian dismissed her question. "Anyway, a report to the SPCA is unnecessary now. Dad was so mad, I thought he was going to go to the police anyway. Now it looks like the animals will be sold, hopefully to good people! Did I tell you that Frisbee and CoCo were picked up this afternoon? And Mr. Zimmer has finally finished building his private stable, so there are 15 guest stalls just waiting to be filled."

"Well, then it will be quiet again in the Bates barn. Hey, Diablo, what are you doing?" Ricki laughed as her black horse stepped over to the donkey, who looked even smaller with Diablo towering above him, and bent his neck down as though he wanted to protect the little gray creature. He began to chew on Chico's mane while the donkey groaned with pleasure. From the beginning Chico had felt at home with all these horses, who must have appeared gigantic to him. At first they looked him over with curiosity, then accepted him into their group.

Diablo poked him gently against the ribs with his nose, and Chico had to spread out his legs quickly to avoid losing his balance.

"Poor little guy," said Ricki with compassion, and Diablo looked at her with his big wise eyes, as though he wanted to say: *This little guy is not poor, he's a lucky guy because he's allowed to stay here...here, where he will have a good life!*

*

Cathy was very nervous. She didn't know if what she wanted to do was the right thing. She kept stopping her bike periodically along the way to think it over.

The last quarter mile to the Bates farm seemed endless. When she rode up the driveway she still had mixed feelings. She had thought – and hoped – that Ricki would be here, but when she saw her bike leaning against the house, Cathy lost her nerve. What would she do if Ricki ignored her? What if Lillian told her to get off the farm? What if?

Dave Bates was coming out the front door just as Cathy had decided to turn around and leave.

"Ah, there's my little lifesaver! You probably want to go see Chico, don't you?"

Embarrassed, Cathy simply nodded and, somewhat reluctantly, let Lillian's father take her to the barn. His daughter and Ricki were just leaving the stable and both were laughing animatedly. When they saw Cathy they stopped in their tracks.

"She actually dared to come here," whispered Lillian hoarsely, and Ricki felt as if she was seeing a ghost. So often she had tried to imagine what it would be like to meet up with her former friend again. At school she had managed to avoid her completely. But that was impossible here.

"You know each other, I think," commented Mr. Bates breezily, although he knew about the breakup of the friendship.

"Dad, this is Cathy...*the* Cathy," Lillian stammered, attempting to make sure her father understood who this girl was. "She and Lark...I mean, the fire at the stable..."

"That's over," he replied firmly, looking from his daughter to Ricki to Cathy. "I don't think she intended to start a fire. And in the end, no one was hurt. Besides, I think she has learned her lesson. Her help yesterday is what counts for me. Maybe it's time to talk it out. You owe that to yourselves after your long friendship, don't you think so?"

Lillian knew her father was right and so she just nodded and hung her head. Ricki stared down at her feet, chastened. She felt worse than she had in a long time. She kept hearing Jake's words: "She was your friend, and she will remain your friend."

Dave Bates took a few steps backward, then turned and walked away from the barn. He could imagine the inner conflict within each of the three girls, but he also knew that he shouldn't meddle now. The kids were old enough to settle this thing by themselves.

Cathy was the first to start.

"I'm so sorry," she said softly, as she looked shyly at Ricky.

Without looking Cathy in the eye, Ricki considered her apology before replying. "Jake has forgiven you. Nothing happened to Diablo. Maybe...maybe..." She looked to Lillian for help and saw that she was nodding her agreement.

"Friends?" Ricki asked Cathy simply but awkwardly.

"Friends! But only if you two want to," the girl's voice cracked and her eyes filled with tears.

"Oh, come here, you silly goose! I'm so glad we're friends again!" Ricki went over to Cathy and took her in her arms for a hug. Then all three girls started to laugh, still a little unsure of themselves, as they entered the barn.

Lillian's father smiled when he saw the trio disappear behind the heavy wooden door.

"I knew it," he mumbled, and began to fill his pipe. He strolled over to the cowshed, lost in thought. Somewhere he had to find a place to stable his daughter's horse as well as Chico. He couldn't let them stay in the barn forever. Besides, the haying was about to begin and he needed every inch of space in the barn. He was glad that, except for Diablo, all the other riding-academy horses had been picked up by their owners. And Ricki's horse would be moving out soon.

*Hmm,* he thought. *Maybe I should talk with the Sulais. After all, they have to renovate their stable anyway. Yeah, I think that might be a good idea.*

*

69

Less than two hours later, Lillian's father had a new problem. Kevin had called and begged him to let him keep a horse in his barn.

"It's Sharazan from the circus. If I can't prove that I have a place to keep him, I won't be allowed to buy him, and Mr. Zimmer's new stable is so expensive. Please, Mr. Bates, it will only be for a little while. I'll find another stable soon. Please. One more horse won't make much difference in your barn."

Lillian's father sighed and surrendered. When he even thought about the malnourished animals at the circus it made his hair stand on end.

"Okay, because it's Sharazan. But it's only a temporary solution!"

"Thank you so much, Mr. Bates. I'll never forget this!"

Kevin bubbled over with excitement. He slammed down the receiver and ran to tell his mother. They didn't dare lose any time. It was already known around the area that Sandro Piccore had to shut down his circus because of financial difficulties. So there were probably other people interested in buying the circus animals.

*

Ricky, Lillian, and Cathy were caught completely by surprise when Mr. Bates told them about Kevin's call.

"This we have to see," they decided quickly, and jumped on their bikes and raced off, while Diablo whinnied quietly after his owner in the barn.

*

70

Sandro Piccore watched with tearful eyes as they loaded his wild animals into the transport cages of the municipal zoo.

Solemnly, the circus family stood in front of the main tent and the ruins of their former life. Although they had often thought about closing down and giving up everything, no one believed that it would ever really happen.

"Just leave already. Get going! I can't bear this anymore!" Natasha yelled at the drivers of the animal transports, then turned abruptly and ran to her trailer.

Juan followed her, his shoulders drooping. He had stayed with his panther until the last minute, stroking its silky coat. He would miss him. For a moment, Juan could feel his rage building.

"You could have at least told us," he hissed at Sandro through tightly pressed lips. But Sandro just shook his head sadly.

"It would have just made everything harder! I had to do this as quickly as possible, before I could change my mind. Believe me, it's better this way, for the animals and for us as well."

"Oh, that's something," sneered Piotr. "All of a sudden? I thought the cir –"

"Oh, shut up!" Rolanda cut off her husband. It hurt her very much to see that it didn't matter to Piotr that her father's life's work was destroyed, gone. It was only yesterday morning, in his trailer, that her father told her of the decision he'd made some time ago.

"We are finished," he had said. He had contacted several zoos and wild animal parks three months before to take the animals off his hands if he couldn't save his circus. That's why everything went so quickly with the transport – all it took was the final phone call.

Sandro, as head of the family, had full control over all the business arrangements for the circus as well as the animals, and therefore the trainers and performers had to abide by his decision.

Since it was a family business, there were no official job contracts, so the artists couldn't force Sandro to continue with the circus by threatening to sue. Besides, if they were honest with themselves, they even felt a little relieved. For the past two years they had really had a hard life.

Rolanda had tried to keep the horses at least, but Sandro remained firm.

"Either all the animals will be sold or none!" he had said, and Rolanda had screamed at him: "I'd rather chase them off then watch someone else take them away!" But even this had not changed anything.

Despite the fact that secretly Sandro would have liked to keep the horses, he stood behind his decision. And so a group of well-to-do riders were standing around Sharazan with calculated expressions on their faces. The sale was like an auction. The offers started with three hundred dollars. After all, they reasoned, why pay a lot of money for this skinny animal. This Piccore should be glad to get anything for him.

Kevin and his mother arrived just as the last offer of eighteen hundred dollars had been raised.

"Mom, please, hurry, before he's sold."

"Two thousand," she said, breathing heavily. She saw right away that Kevin hadn't exaggerated when he described the horse. Sharazan looked almost identical to Leonardo, and he was beautiful. How much better he would look when he had been fed properly.

A fat man with a bald head and a mean grin on his face

turned around and looked straight at Caroline Thomas.

"Twenty-two hundred!"

At that moment, Ricky, Lillian, and Cathy came racing up on their bikes. They left them carelessly leaning against the temporary fence and ran over to Kevin.

"Well, did you get him?" Ricky's eyes were shining, but her friend shook his head.

"Twenty-five hundred," his mother shouted, and Lillian said under her breath, "That's real cheap for this horse."

"Three thousand dollars, but then it's my horse!"

Kevin blanched and turned away.

"It's over!" he whispered. "Mom said we only have twenty-five hundred dollars available. We can't spend any more than that."

Caroline hung her head in disappointment. She felt very sad. She had wanted so much to fulfill this dream of Kevin's, but with the upcoming divorce her financial situation didn't give her any leeway.

Piotr, who was holding the reins of the animal, tried to get them to bid higher by describing Sharazan's best assets. He managed to find another man among the onlookers who was interested, and this one began to bid against the bald man.

Kevin held his hands over his ears, and tears ran down his cheeks. Ricki gave him a hug as Lillian followed the auction, fascinated.

"Thirty-five hundred."

"Forty-five hundred."

"Five thousand dollars!"

With the auction commanding all their attention, the two girls didn't notice that Cathy had disappeared, and Kevin, so upset about Sharazan, hadn't even noticed her there at all.

"Come, let's go," begged Kevin. He took one last long look at Sharazan, who was excitedly dancing on his lead.

"Fifty-two hundred dollars. That's my last offer for this nag!"

Piotr nodded pleasantly to the bald man and held out his hand. The deal seemed to be completed as Rolanda and Cathy suddenly came running up.

"Stop! Just a minute!" shouted Rolanda, waving her arm.

She grabbed the reins out of Piotr's hands, stroked the neck of her horse, and looked doubtfully at Cathy, who was pointing at Kevin. He and the two girls and his mother had already started to walk away.

"Hey!" yelled Rolanda loudly. "Hey, boy! Wait!"

Kevin froze. He felt as though his heart would stop beating.

The young woman started walking toward him with Sharazan, smiled at him sadly, and then gave him the reins.

"I want him to have a good life," she said softly. "Is twenty-five hundred dollars okay? Your friend told me that you lost your horse. Be happy with Sharazan, and be good to my baby!"

Kevin couldn't believe what was happening. He just looked back and forth at Rolanda, the horse, and Cathy, who was timidly standing a short distance away. He had her to thank that Sharazan would now belong to him.

"Thank you," he said, full of emotion; he couldn't say anything more.

"Say, are you crazy?" Piotr's face was bright red with anger. "I already sold him! The nag belongs to that man there!" Rolanda's husband pointed to the mean-looking bald, fat man.

"Fifty-two hundred dollars!" Piotr's eyes sparkled greedily.

"No, only twenty-five hundred, but my baby will have a good life! He's my horse, and I'll sell him! Understood?" Rolanda glared at her husband with such disgust, he didn't dare challenge her.

Kevin's mother took Rolanda's hand and held it between her own. "You've made my son the happiest boy alive," she said, full of feeling. "I promise you that the horse will always be well taken care of." And she removed an envelope with cash from her purse and gave it to Rolanda.

"I know," answered Rolanda, watching Kevin, as he and the girls took turns hugging the horse and each other. Then she saw Sharazan lay his head trustingly on Kevin's shoulder, and she knew that her decision was right.

Slowly and deliberately, with her head held high, she walked back to the tent past Piotr, who was furious about losing twenty-seven hundred dollars.

*Just wait, you'll see what happens!* he thought, and then he, too, ran to the tent, where Rolanda was just bring Rashid out.

Kevin's mother left the grounds pretty quickly. She wanted to see Lillian's parents to discuss the cost of keeping Sharazan in their barn.

Cathy felt almost happy as Kevin hugged her, his shining eyes telling her how grateful he was. She knew she had won back her friends, but still something was weighing on her heart. She glanced at Rashid over Kevin's shoulder and understood how the boy had felt only minutes ago.

Carefully she released herself from Kevin's arms and walked toward the tent. She leaned against the ticket booth and looked wistfully at her dream horse. She felt envious of Kevin and tried to banish those thoughts. She wanted to be happy for him, but she just couldn't get beyond her own sadness.

Rashid had discovered her behind the group of potential buyers and whinnied loudly to her. In one quick moment, he stretched his neck and the reins slid out of Rolanda's hands. Rashid reared, sending the people hurrying out of the way. Then he trotted over to Cathy with a proud head.

The girl held her breath and closed her eyes as the horse blew gently into her hair.

"My good boy," she whispered, hugging Rashid around the neck and forcing herself not to cry. Something indescribable had bound her and this horse together from the beginning, and so it was especially difficult for her to say good-bye to him today.

"Do you want to buy him?" Rolanda had come over to her. She thought she knew how the young girl had been feeling during the last several days.

"There is nothing I would rather do than to buy Rashid, but, unfortunately, I don't have any money." Cathy's voice sounded hoarse and rusty.

Ricky, Lillian, Kevin, and Sharazan had returned to see what had become of Cathy. Together they witnessed an unbelievable scene, one that up until now only happened in books.

An elderly woman approached Rolanda, leaning heavily on her crutches. Without speaking a word, she took in what was happening: Cathy loved this wonderful dun horse and Rolanda needed money and had seen to it that the boy got his dream horse.

The woman closed her eyes for a minute and pictured herself when she was young, wearing a short skirt astride a brilliant white horse.

Carlotta Mancini had been a famous trick rider whose career ended with a serious accident in which she was crippled and her horse killed. When she got out of the hospital, she left the circus, deciding to settle in the lovely countryside near where she gave her last performance – not far from the old brewery. The insurance from the accident – and some wise investments – had made her financially well off, but she had become somewhat of a recluse. Yet whenever a circus toured nearby, she would sit in the audience every day until it left town, and her eyes would shine with joy whenever the horses entered the ring.

"I want to buy this horse," she said to Rolanda, with a further glance at Cathy. She had watched the young teenager during the past few days and had seen how well and lovingly she had taken care of Rashid. "I want to buy him, but not in an auction! You tell me the price, and I will pay it!"

Rolanda turned and looked the well-dressed gray-haired woman in the eyes.

"I know you! Aren't you –?"

"Yes, Carlotta Mancini. So, how much?"

Amazed, Rolanda couldn't stop staring at her. Carlotta Mancini had always been her role model, her idol. She had tried to imitate her riding skills from the time she was six years old, riding on a pony.

"Three thousand dollars," Rolanda answered with a pang of conscience.

"I'll give you five thousand dollars, my child, then with the other horse you will have earned seventy-five hundred dollars! It's hard to find people who are more interested in their animals than they are in the money they can make with them. Here, count it!" Carlotta handed Rolanda a bundle of bills that she had taken out of her coat pocket, all the while never once taking her eyes off Cathy.

Rolanda counted out five thousand dollars and returned the rest to Carlotta.

"Do you have saddles too?" she asked Rolanda, who, still in shock at the apparition before her, could only nod.

"Bring them here. Horses should be ridden and not lead around."

Rolanda sent her two nephews to get the riding gear, and soon two saddles and two shiny snaffles lay on the ground in front of them.

"Wonderful quality," said Carlotta in her smoky voice. "We'll agree on a price later! Then turning to a stunned Cathy said, "So, dear, saddle this horse."

Cathy did as she was told at once.

Ricky, Kevin, and Lillian looked utterly perplexed.

"What's going on here?" Ricki asked quietly, but her friends could only shrug their shoulders. None of them knew what to think of the situation.

"Where are you going to keep your horse?" Carlotta wanted to know from Kevin.

"Well, at first at Lillian's," he said, baffled, and pointed at his friend.

"Aha." Carlotta turned to the girl. "Would it be possible to keep Rashid in your barn as well? Not for free, of course," she added quickly, and Lillian could only nod. She didn't know how she was going to tell her father all this.

"Well, then everything is all set. I just need to know where the stable is so that I can find my horse," she said and laughed. It was a warm and friendly laugh.

"It's the Bates farm. I'm Lillian Bates. We live about two and a half miles in this direction." Lillian pointed to the

78

small woods, behind which her house and farm were located.

"Wonderful, I know where it is." Turning to Cathy, she asked, "So, dear, are you finished? Then get on. You can ride, can't you?"

Cathy, still speechless, could only answer with a nod. She felt as though she were an actress in a film.

*I'm just dreaming.. . It just can't be true,* she thought, as she climbed up on Rashid's high back.

The horse was as gentle as a lamb and remained standing as motionless as a statue. Rolanda has trained him well.

"Do you already have a foster horse?" Carlotta winced a little as she changed her position on the crutches.

Cathy shook her head, this time managing to squeak out a meek, "No."

"Then you have one now!" And while tears of joy ran down Cathy's cheeks as she leaned down to rub her face in Rashid's mane, Carlotta turned to Kevin.

"And what about you? Do you want to run home? Why do you think there is another saddle lying here? I don't need it, that's for sure. So saddle him and then get going. It's time for these horses to be fed properly!"

Kevin couldn't believe what he'd just heard, but when Carlotta pushed the riding gear toward him with her crutch and nodded at him, he understood that she really meant what she said.

As if in a trance, he lifted the saddle and put it on Sharazan's back, then put the snaffle in place.

"Well, then, off you go," Carlotta laughed and stroked Rashid's neck one more time before he trotted away.

"We'll see each other later," she called after the riders, who were escorted by their two friends on bicycles.

# Chapter 5

Sharazan and Rashid had settled in well. Three weeks had passed since Carlotta showed up at Lillian's home to ask her parents if she could board Rashid for a while. Since the horses from the riding academy had already been moved elsewhere, the Bates' said yes, especially as Carlotta was such an incredibly nice, sincere, and funny woman, whose good humor charmed everyone who met her.

Of course, everyone knew that the barn was only a temporary solution, and therefore Dave Bates turned to Marcus Sulai, who was organizing the move into the new house, and offered his carpentry skills to build a new stable.

"It looks like a bomb site at our house! Everything is already packed in boxes, that is, except the coffee machine, which is always in use," Ricki said, looking very tired. The last few days had been strenuous, and she was glad that summer vacation was only one week away.

While Ricki and her friends used the first days of summer to scout the area on horseback, Marcus Sulai had decided to take his vacation now, so that he and his wife could begin fixing up their new home.

Ricki's parents had been at the new house every evening since the Millers moved out. They had painted the walls, papered some, redid the door frames, and laid carpets, so all they had to do when school vacation began was to move their family and their personal belongings in. The two of them had managed to make the old farmhouse look fresh and inviting in an amazingly short time.

Even the little cottage was finished sooner than they had thought possible, and they made it into a cozy space for Jake. Marcus has furnished the little house with the old but lovely pieces of furniture that had belonged to his mother.

"I always knew that we would need them some time," he laughed, glad that he had stored the furniture in the attic after her death.

On the day of the move, Dave Bates arrived at the Sulais' house on a huge tractor with a trailer to help transport their belongings to their new home. But he got there just in time to see a huge moving van turn the corner.

After a few days of arranging the furniture and unpacking, the Sulais were as comfortable in their new home as if they'd always lived there.

Ricki and Harry were happy that they each had a room of their own again and Jake had tears in his eyes as he entered his new home with Lupo under his arm. He had loved the cottage on first sight, but was deeply moved to see how snug and welcoming Marcus and Brigitte had made it.

After a week of settling in they started work on the stable.

Now Dave Bates could really show off his skill as a professional carpenter. In a short time, he had constructed five fabulous horse stalls, better than in most riding schools.

Marcus nodded admiringly as he inspected Lillian's father's work. "Yeah, Dave's a fine craftsman, all right," he grinned, shaking his hand.

Ricki examined all the stalls with excitement. "That's great! The horses can move in today! Super!"

"Take it easy," she was cautioned by Jake. "First we have to get some hay and straw."

"No problem, it's already organized," Dave Bates assured them. "Lillian, Cathy, and Kevin are loading the cart today, and I'm driving them here tomorrow morning."

"What?" Ricki looked a little surprised. "Why didn't anyone tell me? I would have helped."

Lillian's father smiled. "Who would have helped me, then, and done such a good job? No, no, don't worry about it. It won't hurt them to do their part."

Actually, everyone helped to make a wonderful new home for the horses. Before construction began, the adults had gotten together and discussed the plan. With the hay harvest begun, it was time to move the remaining animals out of the Bates' barn so it could be used to store the bales. They all agreed that the Sulais' new stable should be built large enough to house all the horses, including Doc Holliday and Chico.

Dave and Margaret Bates gave them a paddock, which they had built on the meadow between their two properties, Carlotta would pay for the materials necessary to build the stalls, and Jake had declared himself fit enough to handle most of all the work in the stalls. He would finally be back doing what he loved best.

The families would divide all the upkeep costs evenly between them, and since the hay and straw could be bought from Lillian's parents, the monthly expenses wouldn't be too high.

The kids were glad that their horses would be in the same stable, and the adults were very satisfied with the outcome. Even Kevin's mother had learned to laugh again.

The Thomas' divorce was at last finalized, and Carlotta had suggested to Caroline that she and Kevin could move into the separate apartment in her large house, which was only three miles from the Sulais.

"I need someone who can cook, do my housework and the laundry, and go shopping. If you want the job, my dear, you can have it – and don't worry about the rent."

Of course Caroline Thomas said a hearty yes to the offer, and so everyone was in a good mood as they gathered together for a barbecue at the Sulais' to celebrate the stable being finished.

Late in the afternoon, Ricki and her friends, trailed by Harry, ran over to the paddock and, seated on the fence, they watched the silhouettes of their horses glide past them in the dusk.

Ricki was the first one to start to cry a little, and Cathy wiped away a few tears also. Laughing and crying, Diablo's owner called out into the twilight: "I am sooooo happy," and, as though he had understood, Diablo whinnied back.

*

On this night before moving into their new stalls, the horses stayed outdoors in the paddock.

Diablo stood a bit apart from the others and dozed, his head hanging down a little. Suddenly he jerked it upward. The soft squeak of the hinge on the paddock gate had awakened him. Strange, up till now, his two-legged friends had never appeared on the meadow at night.

He sniffed, trying to get a familiar scent, but the light wind was not favorable, and the black horse was unable to

83

recognize anything. For one moment a flashlight lit up the area, but it went out immediately. He heard the squeak again, and then it was quiet all around him.

A little later the wind changed and his sensitive horse nose detected an unpleasant scent. It was the presence of a stranger.

Diablo instinctively felt that something very wrong was happening, and as he started moving closer to the source of the odor, he saw the shadow of an intruder leading Rashid out of the paddock. He whinnied loudly and raced toward the dark figure.

In anger and mistrust, Diablo reared up and kicked at the man, who, cursing at the black horse, dropped Rashid's bridle, stumbled, and fell. He got up swiftly and ran, escaping through the gate, which was now wide open.

Diablo chased the mysterious interloper all over the bordering meadow, until the man suddenly changed direction and ran toward a horse trailer, which was hidden behind a haystack.

Inside the trailer Sharazan kicked against the door forcefully, and as the intruder tried to maneuver backward into the driver's seat without letting the wild black horse out of his sight, Diablo reared up again, and this time struck the intruder on his knee.

Almost unconscious with pain, the man nevertheless managed to start the engine. The trailer rolled backward at first, then sped away with Sharazan locked inside.

Sharazan heard Diablo's hoofbeats as the black horse galloped after the trailer, but the sound of the hoofbeats became softer and softer, and then stopped completely.

*

Diablo stopped running. His flanks quivered and spots of white foam covered his sweaty body. He didn't know how far he had run, but he sensed that he wouldn't be able to catch the horse trailer.

Slowly he lowered his head to the ground. His rage was gone and he longed for a drink of cold water. So turning around, he left the bumpy country road and trotted onto an unfenced meadow, where he quenched his thirst with the dewy night grass. He lay down and rolled around to get rid of the sweat.

When he stood up again he felt a throbbing in his joints. The constant pounding of the hard gallop on the uneven asphalt had caused his joints to swell. Diablo limped a few feet farther and then lay down between two trees to rest.

When dawn came he got up again and trotted stiffly along the road in the direction in which Sharazan had disappeared.

*

Ricki had a direct view of the meadow from her bedroom window, and there was no more wonderful moment in the day than when she opened the window in the morning and heard Diablo's whinny when she called to him.

Every day the noble head of her horse rose when he heard Ricki's voice. He always came as near as possible to the paddock fence and looked at the house impatiently. He knew that within a few minutes his friend would appear with treats.

On this morning Ricki awoke especially early, although she had fallen asleep very late. She was so excited about the horses and the donkey moving into the new stable today that she had a hard time getting to sleep. Sometime during the night, while she was just drifting off, she heard the soft whinny of one of the horses, and she smiled contentedly as she fell asleep.

Awaking in a great mood, she jumped out of bed and opened her window as she did every morning. But as she was about to call to Diablo, the words stuck in her throat.

Ricki's knees went weak and she felt her heart constrict. The paddock was empty!

At first she hoped that Jake, for some reason, had already taken the animals to the stable during the night, but the uneasy feeling in the pit of her stomach told her that something terrible must have happened.

She got dressed quickly, but when she left the house to check the stalls, she saw Chico, who was chewing on a large daisy bush at the edge of a flowerbed. But the horses were nowhere to be seen.

"Oh, my God!" escaped her lips, before Ricki screamed at the top of her voice into the early morning calm, frightening everyone awake.

"The horses! They're gone! Did you hear me? Wake up! Quick, come here!"

Confused faces could be seen at the windows, and then five minutes later the entire Sulai family was gathered around Chico, the only one of the four-legged creatures to be left behind.

Jake arrived out of breath, pale and panting, just as Marcus realized the gravity of the situation and, taking charge, began to give orders. "First we have to tell the others. Brigitte, you start phoning, and ask the Bates' to look at their side of the paddock to see if there's a hole in the fence or if it's broken somewhere. Jake, you and Harry can check out the other side, then we'll know if the animals have broken out or if they—"

Ricki felt her knees wanting to collapse under her.

"Or if they've been stolen! That's what you were going to say, isn't it, Dad?"

Marcus nodded slowly, and Harry ran over to Chico. Gently he put his arm around the thin little donkey and said, "I'm not going to let Chico out of my sight anymore. I don't want him to be stolen too!" Then he took off to find a lead rope.

While Brigitte disappeared into the house to phone the others, Harry came back and hooked the rope to Chico's bridle.

"I'll take Chico back to the paddock," he yelled, and then he ran after Jake with the donkey in tow.

Ricki looked at her father with teary eyes.

"Do you think I'll ever see Diablo again?"

Marcus gathered his daughter in his arms and held her close. "Of course. The horses probably are standing around somewhere nearby. The best thing to do is to start looking around. Your mother can tell the others which direction we went in. So you search this way," he pointed, "and I'll look that way!"

Ricki nodded silently and ran off, worry gripping her empty stomach.

*

"We agreed that you would get both horses! What am I supposed to do with only one horse? You know very well the act only works with both of them!" The man's voice was full of anger, and Sharazan, who always reacted very

87

sensitively to voice tone, pulled his ears back. *Don't come near me,* his behavior warned, and he whinnied menacingly.

"Oh, shut up," hissed another man and kicked against the narrow wooden walls of the shed. A frightened Sharazan kicked wildly, and one of the boards came dangerously loose.

"Be quiet, you stupid horse!" The first man stepped a little to the side. "Why didn't it work out with the second horse! There's nothing simpler than just loading up the horses from the paddock and driving away, is there?"

The other man snorted contemptuously. "It should've been a piece of cake," he said. "I had that one there already in the transporter, and as I ran back to the paddock to get the second horse, a black devil appeared out of the darkness and kicked at me. I fell down and just managed to roll out of the way, when the hooves thundered down just inches from my head. That's a killer, I tell you, a killer – not a horse! Somehow I managed to run away, but that beast followed me to the trailer and almost crushed my kneecap before I could get in."

"Loser! Let's a horse get the better of him!"

"I said, that's a killer…a real devil!"

The man who had ordered the two circus horses stolen walked away from the shed still enraged. If he had known this guy would make such a mess of it, he would have hired a professional. It was too late now; he had to be satisfied with just this one wonderful horse.

*Better than nothing,* he thought. *But this so-called devil…he really interests me.* He sensed that he could earn more money with this unknown black horse than with the two circus animals.

Lost in thought, he turned around and slowly walked back to his old rusty Jeep.

"And what's going to happen to this one?" the thief yelled after his boss.

"Leave him in the shed during the day. Tonight we'll load him up and drive him over the border."

"What if he keeps up this racket?"

"Then you make him be quiet. Tie his mouth shut, hit him, or give him an injection. Do whatever you have to. The main thing is that he's quiet!"

"Great! Why don't you do it? You can see how angry he is, and besides, my leg is injured."

"An injured leg, ha! Maybe we should shoot you like we do when a horse breaks his leg," the boss shouted back, before the Jeep door banged shut and the motor grew loud.

Within a minute or two, the car was hidden behind a hill, and there was nothing to see but the cloud of dust slowly settling to the ground.

The man who was left behind sat down on a large rock in front of the long-abandoned cabin, rubbed his painfully swelling knee, and grumbled.

Inside the shed Sharazan raged. He was thirsty, and today was looking as though it would be terribly hot.

*

Everyone was out searching for the horses. Only Carlotta and Jake sat in front of the Sulais' house and waited tensely to see if someone would turn up with one of the missing animals.

While Carlotta smoked one cigarette after the other, Jake sucked on his already cold pipe. Occasionally they exchanged worried glances.

89

Harry was still holding the rope of the donkey and allowing it to graze. The boy refused to put him into the barn as Jake had suggested.

In order to spare himself another nerve-wracking discussion, Jake let the boy be. Chico would draw him into the shade if it became too hot for him.

Nothing remained of Carlotta's usual jovial manner. The former circus rider had deep worry lines across her forehead, and she nervously beat a rhythm with her crutch against the bench on which she was sitting.

The minutes went by as slowly as hours, and still Carlotta and Jake hadn't said a word to each other. Each was lost in their own dismal thoughts.

"There!" shouted Harry suddenly, pointing down the road. "Someone is coming with a horse! Isn't that Kevin with Holli?"

Jake got up more quickly than one would have thought possible, and even Carlotta pushed herself up with effort.

"A white horse," she called, upset, and Jake squinted his eyes to be able to see better against the sun. Then he nodded and his features started to relax.

"That's Holli. Thank God. If he's here then the others can't be far away! Horses are herd animals."

Carlotta breathed a sigh of relief as well. She was convinced that her dear Rashid would soon be standing with the others in the stable.

*If only I could walk,* she thought in a mix of rage and bitterness before she had to sit down again. But her face brightened when she saw Cathy coming out of the woods with Rashid on a lead. With a big smile, the girl waved animatedly toward the house, and Carlotta, overwhelmed with joy, waved back.

"Darling, now I know why I gave you Rashid to take care of," she said softly, a catch in her voice, as she held out her arms to hug Cathy.

*

Ricki had to sit down and rest. She had grown hoarse from shouting, her throat hurt, and her feet burned as though she had run over glowing coals. She had been running back and forth in the woods for two hours, and it seemed so much larger today than when she had ridden through it. Every few minutes she called Diablo and listened with all her might in every direction to see if she could hear his answering whinny. But, apart from the frightened squawk of the birds and the beating of their wings, the woods were silent.

It was still early in the day, but Ricki was soaking with sweat. In a few hours the sun would be at its strongest, and even in the woods it would be uncomfortably hot.

Inwardly she felt very afraid for her beloved horse, but she was still hopeful that perhaps the others had already found Diablo.

*A cell phone would be a big help right now,* she thought with a sigh, and got up awkwardly. For a moment she wondered whether she should go on searching, but then decided to go back home, making a wide circle over the road.

"Please, God, let Diablo be in the stable when I get back," she prayed, then started jogging home.

*

Ricki was the last one to return to the Sulai house after the search, and Brigitte breathed a sigh of relief when her exhausted daughter came through the door with Kevin.

Of course before going in Ricki had checked the stable to see if all the horses were back, but only Holli, Rashid, and Chico were in their stalls; the other stalls were empty.

She found Kevin sitting on a bale of hay in the corner of the stable with red eyes, staring at the ground.

"Nothing?" he asked when he saw Ricki.

"Nothing at all!" his girlfriend answered, and sat down beside him on the bale. In spite of her exhaustion and awful fear for Diablo, she put her arm around Kevin's shoulder and consoled him.

"They'll come back. I can feel it," she said softly, and Kevin just nodded.

For a few minutes they sat there in silence, giving each other strength, but then Ricki got up, reached her hand to Kevin, and pulled him up.

"Come on," she said. "We have to go see the others. Maybe they've thought of somewhere we can still look."

Together they left the stable and entered the house.

The others all looked at Ricki and Kevin with hope, but all they could do was shrug their tired shoulders and shake their heads.

They got sympathetic looks from Lillian and Cathy, both of whom felt sadness for their friends mixed with relief that their own horses were safe in the stable. Ricki and Kevin tried to smile.

"At least Rashid and Holli are back and safe," the boy said quietly and swallowed hard.

Caroline, Brigitte, and Carlotta exchanged quick glances. The three women were also heavyhearted, but the looks on the faces of the two teens almost broke their hearts.

Brigitte ushered them into chairs and brought them something cool to drink, but as she opened the refrigerator to fetch them some food, Ricki just shook her head.

"Thanks, Mom, but I'm not hungry."

Kevin refused anything as well. He felt as if he would never want to eat again.

Marcus interrupted the heavy silence in the room. "I think it's about time to call the police. Considering the fact that the gate was open and the entire fence is undamaged, I think that someone let the horses out. I mean, I think that...well..."

Ricki became even paler. She reached for Kevin's hand and finished her father's thought: "You mean you think that Sharazan and Diablo have been stolen." She had tried to put this possibility out of her mind since early morning.

"Oh no," Kevin whispered tonelessly, and desperately looked from one person to the another, until his glance stayed with his mother.

Caroline felt as miserable as Kevin looked. She didn't have an answer to her son's unspoken, hopeful question. She just couldn't believe that he had lost another horse.

Jake kept taking his handkerchief from his pants pocket and blowing his nose. Since his birth, Diablo had meant everything to the old man. The idea that his beloved horse was in the hands of criminals was just too awful for him. He felt a slight pain in his chest and made himself stay calm so that he wouldn't risk another heart attack.

Ricki's father took a deep breath and exhaled loudly as he got out of his chair, then left the kitchen to make a phone call.

Ricki downed her glass of soda. She was exhausted and her feet felt as though her shoes were filled with lead. Nevertheless she too got up.

"I'm going back out! I have to find Diablo!"

Kevin got up as well. "I'll go with you!"

As the two started to leave, Carlotta's strong voice held them back.

"Just a minute! You won't get farther than the driveway before you collapse. Ricki, child, you can hardly stand up, and you want to follow horse thieves? Lie down and rest for a half hour. Then we'll get in the car and drive around the area."

"But in a half hour, the horses may be who knows where, and I can't sleep anyway." Ricki tried to protest, but the former equestrienne ignored her objection.

"Who said anything about sleep? If you could sleep now, you wouldn't love your horse. I said you should rest awhile! Remember, we'll be much faster in the car than you two are on foot. And anyway, I don't think the horses are very far away. The thieves know we'll be looking for them, so I think they're close by. They probably have been taken somewhere and hidden, maybe even for a few days, until the search is called off, and then they'll be transported to their actual destination. We have enough time.."

"I'm going to keep looking until I find them," said Kevin rebelliously, and Ricki steadfastly agreed. Nevertheless, because of her painful feet and the summer heat, they decided to follow Carlotta's suggestion. After all, with the car they could search a much larger radius than they could on foot.

Lillian and Cathy put their heads together and whispered earnestly to each other. Then Lillian announced, "The two of us are going to saddle Holli and Rashid later. Maybe they will pick up a scent and lead us to the hiding place."

"Oh, child," said Carlotta, and smiled indulgently. "Believe an old mystery buff when I tell you that is almost impossible! Horses aren't bloodhounds, and the hiding place won't be that close. But you could ride to the nearby farms and ask everyone if they've seen anything unusual."

"And please be careful," warned a worried Margaret Bates. "We don't want anything to happen to you too."

Both girls nodded in agreement, but they thought the adults' fears were completely unfounded. What could happen to them? They would be together, riding two strong, fast horses, and could gallop away from any danger.

*

A few miles north of where he had picked up his search for Sharazan, Diablo left the country road and went into a field. He was now parallel to Echo Lake, very near the riding academy, which had been destroyed by fire.

Before Diablo left the protection of the trees bordering the field, he raised his nostrils to the wind to get a scent. He recognized the smell of a still-smoking campfire. The smoke almost hid the outlines of a tent near the shore of the lake.

Undecided what to do next, the black horse paced back and forth, but his thirst overcame his fears and he approached the lake with trepidation.

A few ducks flew up excitedly as the thirsty horse trotted toward the shore, stepping on twigs lying on the ground, which broke with loud snapping noises.

He drank the water slowly, as though he knew it wouldn't be good for his overheated body if he drank too hastily.

"Hey, what's that? Are there wild horses here?" The loud voice of a youth came from the direction of the tent, and Diablo jumped aside, frightened.

"Come on, let's catch him! Yippee, just like in the Wild West!"

Diablo laid his ears back and whinnied shrilly. He reared up imposingly and turned around 180 degrees to dash back to the safety of the woods. While he was galloping away, he heard the sound of three motorcycles hot on his trail.

The three riders knew how to maneuver their all-terrain bikes well, and it was impossible for Diablo to outrun them.

The young men chased Diablo into the underbrush and then surrounded him in an old quarry, circling him with their bikes, until the horse panicked and began turning around and around, trying to find a way out – but to no avail.

# Chapter 6

Ricki and Kevin sat silently in Carlotta's car, dazed and numb with worry.

The policeman, who showed up at the Sulais' house after Marcus called, took down the complaint that two horses had been stolen, but informed the family that the police couldn't intervene until it was clear that the horses had actually been taken.

"After all, the two other horses have come back and the donkey is in the stable. It could very well be that the two missing horses are still in the area, trotting around free. Also, it's possible you forgot to close the gate."

"And what does that mean?" Marcus asked defensively.

The policeman flipped his notebook closed and returned it to his back pocket.

"That means that we have to wait 48 hours to see if the horses come back. Only if they're still missing after this time frame can we assume that there's been a crime. Sorry, there's nothing we can do now. These animals like to take off, and the owners are normally responsible for catching them, unless the animals are endangering traffic. But that's not very likely out here in the country, since the only people who regularly drive on these roads are the people who live here, and they know it's possible that an animal may be on the road at any time."

Then he nodded and tipped his cap to the group, said good-bye, and left before any more questions could be asked. He left behind disappointed and incredulous faces.

On the way back to the station, he could still see Ricki's pleading look, and he decided to drive around the area in his own car and keep his eyes open after he got off work at 2 p.m. His instincts told him their assumption that the horses had been stolen was correct.

Carlotta drove fairly fast. She figured the thieves had driven north to the next large town, thinking that their trail, if it were found, would be lost more easily there than in the country. Marcus Sulai and Dave Bates had gone south to further their earlier search in that direction. The question was, which way did the thieves go?

"If only we knew what we're looking for," said Ricki, who was sick with anxiety. "A horse trailer? An animal transport truck? A stable?"

"We'll just have to pay attention to everything and anything," answered Carlotta staring grimly out the window. If this had been a mystery novel, she probably would have known already who the thieves were and where to find the horses. Her expertise in solving detective stories enabled her to figure everything out after the first few chapters. But this wasn't a story, it was rock-hard reality, and that was completely different.

Silence returned to the car as the driver and passengers resumed their own private thoughts.

*

"At least we can store the tents and park our trailers here until we know what we're going to do," said Rolanda casually to Piotr, who was limping up the steps to their trailer behind his wife.

Sometimes, when they were putting up the large tents or taking them down, the huge masts would get out of control and fall over, injuring one or more of the workers.

Rolanda glanced at her husband's leg.

"You should go see the doctor."

"Leave me alone," grumbled Piotr. He was still angry because Rolanda had sold the horses against his wishes.

"You made me look like an idiot! You made me a laughingstock! Don't ever do that again! Do you hear me?" Furious, he went into the bathroom and began to change his clothes. Moments later he reappeared and, pushing wordlessly past Rolanda, stormed out of the trailer.

"Where are you going now?" she asked angrily, following him outside.

"To a bar!" he yelled back. And gunning the engine of his car, he drove off the brewery grounds, tires screeching.

"I told you from the beginning that you wouldn't be happy with him," said Sandro softly behind Rolanda, and gently laid his hand on her shoulder.

"When everything is over and cleared up, I'm going to divorce him," answered Rolanda calmly, although inside she was upset and angry.

Sandro nodded his approval, and slowly father and daughter walked off. Without another word exchanged between them, they walked onto the bordering field, each thinking about the future. Neither knew what the circus family would do after they left here. Only that Piotr wouldn't have any part in Rolanda's life. That much was certain.

Rolanda's thoughts turned to Rashid and Sharazan. She wondered how they were. She linked her hand under her father's arm and smiled sadly at him. It had never been clearer to her how glad she was that this man was on her side.

*

"You darned beast!" The man had just tried to put a bucket of water into the dark shed for Sharazan, but the horse was so frightened by his sudden entry, and so blinded by the light that rushed through the opened door, that he snapped at the intruder.

The man screamed and dropped the bucket, rubbing his painful arm.

"As far as I'm concerned, you can die of thirst," hissed the dark figure. "I'm not bringing you anything else, even if Brady takes my head off! You're not worth it. I'm not risking becoming an invalid because of you! Do you understand me? YOU'RE NOT WORTH IT!"

He spat on the floor in front of the animal and stomped out. In his anger he kicked the wooden door, and with a loud bang and a creak in the hinges it fell shut.

Sharazan kicked against the narrow walls surrounding him. He was sweating in his dank prison. Thirst was making him crazy, and his tongue was already swollen. He bit into top layer of the wall boards and his legs began to shake.

He knew that he wouldn't be able to stand this oppressive heat much longer. He was exhausted, depleted of mineral, yet he couldn't even lie down. The narrow wooden walls forced him to remain standing.

Desperate, the horse tried to rear up, to free himself, but

he bumped his head on one of the low ceiling rafters. He screamed in pain, and then, finally numb, stood very still.

The man heard the horse's scream of pain but didn't react, except to show a nasty grin. "You deserved it," he sneered. Impatiently he looked at his watch every few minutes, but time was passing very slowly.

"At least eight more hours until it's dark," he groaned to himself. He wiped the sweat off his forehead. The sun felt hotter than ever.

He shuffled over to the large rock where he had stored a few bottles of beer in its shadow. He pulled one out, opened it, and drank the tepid brew greedily, while Sharazan's head sank lower and lower.

"Cheers, you beast!" his tormentor laughed loudly. He finished off the rest of the beer, lay down, pulled his hat over his eyes, and dozed.

*

Lillian and Cathy had saddled Holli and Rashid and rode off despite the heat and knowing better. They left Chico in the stable braying forlornly for his four-legged friends.

This was the second time today that they all had left him alone. Fortunately Harry was still there, and he sat right down in the donkey's stall and tried to comfort him with lots of carrots.

Without thinking about it, the two girls had started off in the same direction as Carlotta. They made good progress and looked in every direction to see if they could find the missing horses. They stopped at every farm and house they came to, asking everyone to keep their eyes open for Diablo and Sharazan. Then they continued on their way focused and determined.

After about an hour and a half, they began to feel the beginnings of sunburn on their faces and shoulders, and they turned into the nearby woods to protect themselves from the sun's rays in the shadows of the trees.

"What do you think?" asked Lillian, taking out her bandanna and mopping the sweat from her face, "Should we make a little excursion to Echo Lake? It's very near here. We could let the horses drink, and I think we could use a little cool water on our faces too."

Cathy agreed at once. "Good idea! I think I could jump in with all my clothes on!"

The girls changed their direction again, having no idea that they were on the same path Diablo had been on only a few hours earlier.

"Look, there are some campers over there!" Cathy pointed to the clearing at the edge of the lake.

"Let's ask them if they saw anything," suggested Lillian, as they watched the three young men in motorcycle dress take down their tent.

"I don't I like the looks of them," said Cathy to her friend, who was two years older, as they rode nearer.

"You don't have to go to the movies with them," replied Lillian. Then she gathered her courage and approached the men, who were looking at the girls on horseback with suspicion.

"Excuse me," called Lillian from a safe distance. "Excuse me, but have you by any chance seen two horses running about free? A black one and a roan with a long mane and a long tail?"

The men nervously looked at each other. Then the oldest looking one of the group limped forward with a broad grin.

"Hey, girls, how about tying up your horses and coming for a ride with us on our bikes?"

Cathy blushed with embarrassment and looked away, but Lillian didn't let it bother her.

"Someone stole two horses from us last night, and we're looking for them."

She noticed that the dark young man standing behind the speaker seemed a little more jittery than the others.

"Stolen?" the oldest one asked. "I see. Well, we haven't hidden them in our tent!"

"I didn't say you did; I just asked, if –"

"And we haven't seen anything either, isn't that right?" He turned to face his buddies with a warning glance, and the rest of them shook their heads.

"Well, girls, sorry. I guess that's it! Maybe your horses are already in the glue factory," he joked mean-spiritedly.

Lillian and Cathy blanched, and after a frightful moment turned around and galloped back into the woods, where they felt safer.

"That was a horrible guy," panted Cathy, out of breath. "I wouldn't like to run in to him in the dark."

Somewhat more composed now, they continued their search, riding on slowly. About half an hour later they heard the sound of a motorcycle behind them. Scared, the girls lead their horses away from the path and into a clearing and then watched as the lone biker stopped, took of his helmet, and started frantically waving at them.

Hesitantly, the two girls rode toward the biker until they recognized the dark young man from the group.

"I'm…I'm sorry about what my friend said a while ago," he said, sounding ill at ease. Hesitantly he added, "Yeah, well, we did see a horse. It was large and black."

103

"Diablo!" Lillian rode up so close to the young man that he could almost feel Holli's breath on his face. Respectfully, he let his bike roll back a little before he continued.

"It appeared at the lake, and Butch said we could play a little 'Wild West.'"

"And then?" Lillian's eyes flashed threateningly. She suspected something bad.

"Then, well, we started to chase the black horse on our bikes."

"You chased him?"

"No…we…yeah. We chased him for almost an hour. I never thought a horse could run that fast for so long."

Lillian and Cathy were very distressed at what they had just heard. They dreaded what else the young man would tell them.

"Well, then, we followed him to the old quarry."

"Come on, quit stalling! What happened then?"

The conversation was very uncomfortable for the biker. When he thought back to the time in the quarry, he felt guilty about taunting the black horse. That was the reason he'd left his two companions and rode after the girls.

"Well, we…we surrounded the horse and rode around him a few times. Butch wanted to scare him and rode toward him. But the horse reared up on his hind legs and when he came down he hit Butch with his hooves. Then Butch got mad and drove the horse toward the cliff. The horse climbed up a few feet but then he started to slide and…"

"And what?" Cathy thought her heart would stop beating.

"Well, he fell down and just lay there."

"We…" the young man looked down at the ground in shame, "we just rode away."

"You did what? How could you be so cruel to chase a defenseless animal – and then just let it lie there! Where is he now?"

The biker shrugged his shoulders. "No idea. I guess he's still lying there."

Lillian felt an unbelievable rage boil inside her. She would have liked to report this guy to the police right then, but time was short and they needed to get to Diablo and help him. So she turned Holli in the direction of the quarry and galloped after Rashid, while the biker raced in the opposite direction and hoped that the girls hadn't made a note of his license plate.

\*

"I think we should turn around," said Carlotta, just as Kevin pointed excitedly out of the window.

"Look – over there – isn't that Holli and Rashid? Man, are Lily and Cathy completely crazy, riding like that?"

Way off Ricki saw two riders galloping at full speed through the field. Carlotta had to concentrate on her driving and, besides, she wasn't far-sighted enough to recognize anything that distance away. She asked nervously, "Are you sure?"

"Well, I'm not positive," replied Ricki. "But if it is them, then they'll have a good reason for racing the horses in this heat. Normally they would never do such a thing!"

Carlotta pushed the gas pedal almost to the floor, and her Mercedes took off as if it had wings, heading in the direction of the two riders. Stones flew up and hit the underside of the car, and Kevin was afraid that the bottom would be covered with holes by the time they arrived. But Carlotta didn't seem to care. She just kept her foot on the gas pedal and raced to catch up with the riders.

Ricki, who was hanging on to Kevin for dear life, suddenly yelled, "I know! I know where they're going! They're heading for the old quarry. I can't imagine why they want to go there? It's very dangerous." She looked questioningly at Kevin, but he had no idea either and just shrugged his shoulders. Gradually he was getting more and more sick to his stomach – and it wasn't because of Carlotta's driving. It was fear for Sharazan and Diablo!

Ricki also sensed that something was very wrong, and she began to tremble and wring her hands. She stared at the two girls, who were now just reaching the bar that lay across the entrance to the old quarry.

They brought their horses to a standstill, their hearts beating rapidly. They looked around from astride their horses, but there was no Diablo lying on the ground as they had imagined in horror.

Cathy and Lillian sprang out of their saddles, and with trembling knees led their steaming horses slowly along the inner boundary of the quarry. They stared carefully at the ground, searching for tracks.

"Darn it!"

The motorcycle tracks were clearly visible, but Diablo's hoof marks were no longer distinguishable from the hoof marks of their own horses.

As Carlotta pulled her car up in front of the barrier, Holli and Rashid jumped in fright. The girls were jolted as well. With relief they recognized Ricki and Kevin, who were running toward them.

Carlotta got out of the car awkwardly. With her crutch

for support, she walked toward the young people. Rashid whinnied happily as he recognized his owner. While Carlotta stroked her horse's neck tenderly, Lillian and Cathy exploded with all that had happened.

"…and then we rode here as fast as we could and hoped that we would find Diablo."

"I'm glad you didn't find him, that means he survived the fall from the cliff." Ricki had tears in her eyes, and she had to work hard to keep from sobbing out loud when she thought of all the things that could have happened to her horse.

"We're going to search every inch of this quarry. There has to be some clue about Diablo somewhere," decided Carlotta, and limped off to look for it.

Each of the others took a different part of the area, and soon their eyes were sore from the glare of the sun and the effort of searching for any sign of Ricki's beloved horse.

The air shimmered, and the search party longed for some shade and a chance to rest, but the thought of Diablo kept them looking.

Suddenly Kevin began to wave frantically for them to come to him.

"Over here! Come on! I think I found something!"

Ricki was the first to reach her friend, and for one moment she thought she was going to faint. Taking a few deep breaths to steady herself, she carefully knelt down and examined a few stones. They appeared to be covered with drops of dried blood.

"My God, he's injured!"

Helplessly she looked up at the others, then abruptly got to her feet. As calmly as she could she said, "If he's bleeding, then there should be more of these signs, and when we find them, we'll have a trail!"

Carlotta nodded excitedly. She had hoped the search would go like this. The five of them stared back at the ground, and slowly, stone by bloody stone, they followed Diablo's trail out of the quarry and onto the road, where the trail ended.

"We need a bloodhound," said Cathy, but Carlotta rejected the idea.

"Where could we find a bloodhound now? No, no, time is too precious. At least we know the direction to continue the search. Lillian, Cathy, get back in the saddle and ride through the field toward the woods. We'll drive the car along the road. You can look around in the woods better on horseback, and we'll look all around here. I'm not sure, but I have a strange feeling we're on the right path!"

"Okay, madam detective," Lillian said, and in spite of the tension in the situation, they all managed a slight smile. They hoped they were finally getting close to finding their horses.

# Chapter 7

Officer Hank Gordon drove around Echo Lake in his old Volvo. He had finished his shift with the police for the day when he heard about the illegal camping out by the lake and told his colleagues he'd drive by after leaving the station and see what was going on.

Of course, when he arrived there was nothing left to see of the campers except for the smoking campfire, which was a mute witness to their presence.

Shaking his head with annoyance, the officer made sure that all the coals were out. He didn't understand how people could be so irresponsible as to set a fire on the edge of the woods and then not put it out completely when they left, even if there was a source of water nearby.

As he walked back to his car he noticed hoof marks next to the motorbike tire tracks along the lakeshore, and immediately he remembered the report of the stolen horses.

A glance at his watch told him that he still had about two hours before he had to show up to coach Little League – time enough to look for the horses. However, he decided to stop by to see the Sulais first to make sure that the horses weren't already safe in their stalls.

On the way to the farm, an expensive-looking car sped by him, passing much too fast.

"Well, that's just not okay," mumbled Hank Gordon to himself. Stepping on the gas, he tried to overtake the speeding car, but his Volvo didn't have a chance against Carlotta's Mercedes. As the distance between the two cars increased, he could only jot down the license number. Later he'd find out who the driver was.

*

Diablo was exhausted. His joints ached, and his left hind leg especially was giving him trouble. The wound on his ankle, which he had gotten as a result of the fall in the quarry, had stopped bleeding, but it was covered by flies and mosquitoes, and they were driving the horse crazy. Diablo kept kicking out in order to get rid of them, but the dried blood and his sweat served as a magnet for the insects, and they continually swarmed around him.

The flight from the bikers had driven him a far distance, and he was in a location he had never been before with Ricki in the saddle. Still, he thought he recognized the dilapidated water tower on top of the hill in front of him. It must have been before Ricki's time that a rider had visited the area with him.

Diablo decided to climb the hill to get a better view of the area. Carefully he put one hoof in front of the next until he had reached the tower ruins.

He was happy to find that the grass and herbs up there were much greener and juicier than those growing in the valley. He bent his neck down to graze before continuing on his way. He ate well, knowing that it may be a long while before he would find food again.

110

After some time, a noise startled him, and he raised his head and flexed his ears back and forth. Hadn't he just heard the neighing of a horse in the distance?

There it was again! Excitement surged through Diablo's body.

He paced nervously back and forth, trying to pick up the scent of the other horse. Then he stopped and stood still with his tail held majestically high, before his answering neigh echoed over the fields.

For Sharazan, who was still imprisoned in his shed, Diablo's call, which he heard from a great distance, sounded like a rallying cry, urging him not to give up. New strength seemed to pulse through the body of the circus horse. He began to neigh in ever shorter intervals, to show Diablo the way.

*

When Hank Gordon drove onto the grounds of the Sulai farm, he could hardly believe his eyes. An elderly woman was just getting out of the very car he had been following – the same woman he had met at the Sulais' this morning on his official visit to check on the reported horse theft.

"Lady," he called and waved to her as he sprang out of his car. "Lady! You know, of course, that you just drove past me at 100 miles an hour!"

Carlotta looked him up and down and then put on her friendliest smile. "Young man, you should have your tachometer checked. It was exactly 120 miles an hour!" With great dignity she limped past him on her crutches, but after only a few steps she turned around to the policeman, now in civilian clothing.

"By the way, the horses are still missing. And if you think you have to follow anyone, then start with the three bikers who chased one of the horses into the old quarry, and, when it tumbled down a slope, left it lying there alone and rode away."

Officer Gordon raised an eyebrow. "I'll follow up on that for sure, if you can prove what you just said is true. Nevertheless, you were driving too fast – much too fast – and I'm forced to –"

"Oh, do whatever you want," Carlotta interrupted with impatience, waving him away and heading back toward the house. "I don't have time right now for a lecture. The life of these horses and finding them is very important to me, and we're going to continue our search and I won't let you stop me! If you had done something about it this morning, I wouldn't have had to drive as though I had been bitten by a tarantula! By the way, your proof is just arriving on horseback. Ask the girls!" Carlotta pointed to Lillian and Cathy, who were slowly approaching the Sulai farm.

Unable to find any other traces of Diablo, the two had decided to return, walking their horses the rest of the way to avoid exerting them any further in the summer heat.

Gordon jotted down some notes while the girls took care of the horses and told him what had happened. Then the policeman took out his cell phone and called his precinct. Finally he had some tangible information to go on. He would question the bikers about their illegal camping and chasing of Diablo – if he could find them. After passing the details on to his colleagues, he got back into his car and drove away. He wanted to inspect the old gravel quarry himself. Maybe he would find a useful clue there.

*

"Don't be angry with me," Rolanda said, turning to her father, but I'd like to walk a little farther by myself. It's so beautiful here, and I'd like to think over some things. "She paused in thought for a moment. "Do you know what?" she asked, glancing around. "I'm wondering if I should stay here. It doesn't really matter where I look for a job, and this place is as good as any other."

Sandro wrinkled his brow. "Is it possible that you want to stay here because of your horses – to be near them?"

The young woman shrugged her shoulders. "Maybe. I don't know. After all, they aren't 'my' horses anymore."

Sandro shifted his gaze away from his daughter. He didn't want her to see the guilt in his eyes for having that her animals be sold. But he knew that she would have more possibilities if she weren't encumbered by them. Several members of his circus family had already left, looking for and jobs elsewhere. It would be more difficult for him, he wasn't young anymore.

"I'll see you later," he said, and walked on alone.

"Ciao," Rolanda called after him, and continued her walk.

The heat didn't seem to bother her. She just kept on walking. *Where would the horses be boarded? What had the youth said? What was the girl's name?* Rolanda sighed. She was angry with herself that she hadn't paid more attention when Carlotta was talking to the young people. All she knew was that Lillian had pointed in a vague direction and had said something about two and a half miles.

As much as Rolanda enjoyed walking, it would have been quicker if she had taken the car. Her anger at Piotr, who had taken the car, returned, and, as if in instant replay, her life with him passed before her eyes.

She kept asking herself why she had married the man. He wasn't attractive, he didn't have a good character, and he wasn't worth much.

After much soul searching, Rolanda came to the conclusion that Piotr had married her at a time when Sandro and the circus were doing well. After all, by marrying the owner's daughter he gained a certain amount of security and perhaps he thought that one day the circus would be his. So Rolanda looked like a pretty good catch.

Before they were married he was respectful and attentive. It was only after the wedding that he showed his true character. The brutality that resulted from his fits of rage became a problem for the whole family, as well as for the animals. Nevertheless, not much was said about it. He was a part of the family now and they had to stick together.

Lost in thought, Rolanda took a wrong turn and went farther and farther away from the Bates farm without knowing it.

*Two and a half miles can't be that far,* she thought, and sat down on a tree stump to rest for a few minutes.

She tried hard to find something she recognized, so that she would know where she was, but nothing looked familiar. Recently she had often taken walks around the old brewery because she had decided to visit her former horses, but after a short while she had always turned back to spare herself the pain of seeing them again.

But today the entire area seemed unfamiliar to her. Looking around in every direction, the only thing she noticed was a run-down Jeep about 100 yards away, and that it was raising a huge cloud of dust from going so fast. Soon it disappeared around a bend in the road.

Rolanda had a feeling she knew that car from somewhere and, strangely, the feeling made her very uneasy. Her senses sharpened. Up until now she associated this feeling of uneasiness only with her horses. Every time there had been anything wrong with Sharazan or Rashid, her so-called sixth sense kicked in and she felt like this. Whether it had been colic or one of the horses had gotten caught in the chains used to tether them, she had always followed her feelings and was able to help them in time.

What if one of the horses was sick or in danger now? Her discomfort grew until she was sure that something was very wrong.

Suddenly Rolanda felt a deep urge to walk in the same direction the car was heading. She was convinced the road would lead her to the right farm. So she turned and started walking back in the direction from which she came.

*

Ricki and Kevin were devastated. They had hoped so much to find their horses while driving around, but, unfortunately, had no such luck.

Now they were sitting on Ricki's bed, exhausted, their backs leaning against the cool wall and their knees drawn up to their chests. Both stared at their feet, too tired to talk or even cry. They felt burned out, empty, and, most especially, helpless.

"I'll never ride again," said Kevin, breaking the silence, his voice barely above a whisper.

"How come?" Ricki responded automatically, not really taking in what Kevin had said.

"What do you mean, 'How come?'" Kevin sounded irritated.

Ricki sighed and looked at her boyfriend.

"Please, excuse me, I wasn't listening. What did you just say?"

"Just forget it!"

Once again they sat in silence. After a few minutes someone knocked softly on the door, and Harry stuck his head in the room.

"Mom wants to know if you –"

"NO!" they both yelled together, before the little boy had even finished what he was going to say.

"But you don't even know what –" he tried again, but Ricki cut him off again.

"Harry, leave us alone!"

Ricki's brother too a step back, looking hurt and offended. Quietly he left, closing the door behind him. But two minutes later he flung it open with a bang. Ricki was just about to scream at him again, but Harry was faster this time. Tears rolled down his cheeks, as he yelled, "Why are you screaming at me? I didn't do anything. It's not my fault that your horses were stolen. And…and…I'm sad, too, that Diablo and Sharazan aren't here. Especially now that they have such a wonderful stable."

Seeing her little brother in such emotional distress made Ricki feel even worse.

"Harry, we are just so tired from looking for them and so worried about them," she said, trying to justify her behavior.

"So what?" sobbed Harry. "I'm worried too, but I'm not yelling at anyone! And I'm tired too. I took care of Chico all day, just so you know!"

Ricki eased herself off the bed and gave her little brother a hug. Suddenly feeling very protective of him, she held him close and stroked his head.

"You're right, Harry," she said softly. "I'm sorry I yelled at you. And I think it's really great that you took such good care of Chico. I'm very proud of you."

Harry looked up at her. "Honest?" he asked doubtfully.

"Scout's honor!" answered Ricki, putting her hand over her heart.

"Are you two coming downstairs now? Mom made hot dogs, and she says you have to eat something, otherwise you're going to peel over!"

Harry's blooper broke through Kevin's gloom, and he burst out laughing. "You mean 'keel over.'"

"Oh. So are you coming?"

Ricki kissed Harry on the top of his head and gently pushed him out the door. "Tell Mom we'll think about it," she said.

Kevin stared at the closed door, reflecting. "I always wanted to have a brother. Are we going?"

"Do you really want to?" asked Ricki.

Kevin nodded. "Your mother is right. I'm not really hungry, but a hot dog wouldn't be the worst thing. Anyway, it makes no difference to the horses if we eat or not."

"If you think so," replied Ricki, and then she heard her stomach growling. "That's two to one! Okay, let's go," she said, although she didn't feel at all hungry.

*

"So, are you two okay?" Marcus asked the young couple when they joined the others in the kitchen. He knew the fears in his daughter's heart, as well as in her friend's, but he saw that they had themselves under control – at least it looked like that at the moment. What it was like when they were alone together was a completely different thing.

117

"We're going to keep looking afterward, aren't we?" Ricki asked nervously and looked in the faces of each of the adults present for some encouraging message.

For a moment everyone seemed to be thinking it over, and then Brigitte began cautiously, "Well, I think now that the police are showing some initiative, maybe we should let them handle it. After all, we have no idea where to look for the horses."

"But Diablo was in the quarry!"

"Yeah, but what about Sharazan? We haven't heard anything about him, much less seen him."

"Another reason to go on looking," intervened Carlotta. Her words were accompanied by Kevin's thankful nodding.

"I would help you look for them, but I can't do everything I would like to do anymore," added Jake, his voice tight. He seemed to be furious with himself, his age, and his weak heart.

Caroline Thomas glanced from her son to Ricki and back to her son. "Well, I can understand your being restless as long as the horses are missing, but you were out in the hot sun for several hours already today. Maybe it would be better to let the police take over. They know best what to do in such –"

"Mom!" Kevin shouted, tossing her a look of disappointment. "Mom! Sharazan has been stolen, Diablo was chased by a motorcycle gang, and you're worried that we might get too much sun!"

"Exactly! Kevin, if you and Ricki get sun poisoning, we'll be the ones to take care of you, and the horses still won't come back any sooner."

A frustrated Jake banged his fist on the table. " The police can only look for them, and we don't know if they are even doing that," growled Jake. "If only I was a little bit younger," he added remorsefully, and looked at Marcus. "You young people have cars, strength, and perseverance. Use them. It's not two old earrings that are missing, it's two wonderful horses – your children's horses – they're part of the family! Would you sit here calmly eating dinner if Ricki and Kevin were in the hands of kidnappers?"

"Jake, I think you're exaggerating just a little. There's a difference between a person being kidnapped and a horse being stolen!" Dave Bates tried to calm Jake down a little, but he only made it worse.

"It's easy for you," the old man replied. "Your Doc Holliday is uninjured and safe in his stall, your donkey too. How would you react if Lillian's horse were missing? If you saw how miserably unhappy your daughter was? Don't you think it would hurt you badly to see your child suffer? Wouldn't you do anything to find Holli? Anyway, you, the man who went to the circus and got into a fight to save a donkey – a donkey that didn't mean anything to you!" Jake got himself so worked up he started to cough, and then pressed his hand to his chest.

"Don't get excited, Jake, do you hear me?" Marcus put his hand on Jake's shoulder to calm him. "You're right Diablo is part of our family and Sharazan is part of Kevin's. We'll keep looking!"

The old stable master, tired from his outburst, nodded with satisfaction and leaned back heavily in his chair.

Ricki and her friends were relieved. They were worried the adults would get into a fight.

"Well," said Carlotta, who was nibbling potato chips as she mulled everything over, "we have to assume that the

119

horses are not together. After all, the bikers mentioned only Diablo, didn't they?" She looked at Lillian and Cathy when she asked the question, and they nodded affirmatively. "Well, that could mean that only Sharazan was stolen, and that probably Diablo, like Rashid and Holli, ran out of the paddock. It's strange that the three horses didn't stay together. There must be another reason." She continued to think out loud. "On the other hand, I ask myself was Sharazan really stolen or did he simply run out of the paddock in another direction. However," she added after a momentary hesitation, "however, he probably would have gone with Rashid, they've been together for years. But my intuition tells me that someone took him, because we haven't seen or heard anything from him, and at least we have some clues about the whereabouts of Diablo."

The brain of the self-appointed detective was working overtime. Carlotta tried to imagine all the possibilities that would explain the disappearance of the horse, and was worried that she had forgotten something or overlooked some clue.

Raising his hand as if he were in school, Harry asked in all innocence, "How can you just take a big horse with you?"

"Very simple," answered Ricki easily. "Open the horse trailer, put the horse inside, shut the horse trailer, and bye-bye!"

Impressed by Harry's perceptive question – and Ricki's answer – Carlotta's face brightened.

"Hey, kids, you're really good...no, you're geniuses! That's exactly it! We just spent a lot of time driving around, hoping to see one of the horses or a transporter or a truck that was standing around or driving around this area. But we haven't looked near the paddock to see if maybe tracks from the tires or something are visible. After all, the transporter can't have been parked too far away, otherwise the risk of being seen during the theft would have been too great. On the other hand, it had to be far enough away from the farms so that no one would be awakened by the noise as it drove away in the night."

Carlotta was on a roll. She was confident they were getting closer to the heart of the mystery. At the time, however, no one knew just how close the former circus performer was to the actual facts.

Kevin and Ricki exchanged admiring glances.

"Wow, Carlotta, that could be exactly how it happened."

"And? What do we do now, after realizing how it could have happened?"

"Should we tell Officer Gordon?"

"Do you have any idea where he is at the moment?"

"No!"

"Exactly!"

The kids all talked excitedly at once, and Harry, Jake, and their parents looked to Carlotta for advice.

"Well, Detective Mancini, what do you suggest? How should we proceed?" Lillian's father asked, hardly bothering to hide his smile.

"Harry – get the car!" she ordered, just like the detectives in the movies and on TV.

"What am I supposed to do?" the youngster jumped up ready to help. Everyone laughed. The tension was broken.

"Not you! Him!" his mother chuckled, pointing to the man sitting next to him.

"But his name is Dave!"

"Yes, my darling. You heard what Carlotta said: Dave – get the car!"

Dave Bates wiped his mouth with a napkin and got up. "Yes, that's exactly what I'm going to do. And then we'll look all around the paddock. Maybe we'll be lucky and find a clue."

One after the other, they each stood up, anxious to get back on the case. Only Jake and Harry remained seated.

"I'll stay with Chico, Holli, and Rashid in the meantime!" announced the little boy importantly.

"Well, then I'll take care of you!" Jake said, acknowledging the importance of the task Harry took on himself.

"Good luck," he wished the others, who were headed to the door, in a hurry to get going. Thanks to Carlotta's sharp logic they had a new perspective on the mystery and a renewed commitment to solving it.

"Thanks," they shouted in unison, "see you later." In the kitchen Jake and Harry heard the first of the car doors slam shut in the driveway.

\*

Officer Hank Gordon had inspected the quarry more closely. His trained eyes had discovered the tracks of the motorcycles on the stony ground rather quickly. Deeply embedded in one of the tire tracks he found a cigarette lighter with the logo from the Red Moon Café-Bar on it, which one of the bikers had probably dropped while chasing the horse.

The policeman took a clean handkerchief and a little plastic bag out of his pocket, picked up the lighter with the cloth and maneuvered it into the bag. For all he knew, it might have fingerprints of the criminals on it. He wanted to clear that up at the crime lab soon, but he decided to visit the café-bar first to find out if anyone knew anything about the motorcyclists. Perhaps someone was acquainted with those losers or, maybe, with a little luck, they would be there. Thanks to the detailed description from Lillian and Cathy, he was sure he would recognize them right away.

Officer Gordon ducked back under the barrier, got into his car, and drove off in the direction of the Red Moon. Since he didn't want to lose any time, he decided to take the shortcut through the woods, totally forgetting that he was no longer on duty and expected at the ball field to coach.

# Chapter 8

Rolanda began to feel the muscles in her legs tighten. She was used to a lot of physical activity, but the long walk on the hard ground in thin-soled shoes was tougher on her body than she had thought. Nevertheless, she kept on walking, while the feeling of dread got stronger and stronger the farther she went.

She stopped for a moment to massage her right calf. A leg cramp was coming on. While she was rubbing her calf, a fleeting movement made her glance at the ridge of trees at the far side of the field.

What was it that kept appearing and then disappearing between the trees?

Rolanda wrinkled her brow and squinted.

*That's impossible,* she said to herself, baffled. *That's a horse running free. I think I'm starting to hallucinate!*

She straightened up quickly, left the road, and started to jog across the field toward the animal, although she didn't really think she could overtake it, much less catch it. It probably would disappear before she even reached the edge of the field that bordered the row of trees. But she kept running anyway, paying no attention to her weary legs, driven by the feeling that there was a reason why she had come across the horse.

At last she came to the edge of the field, where she stopped, exhausted. Just as she had thought, the animal had disappeared, and everything seemed peaceful. Bending over with hands on her thighs, trying to catch her breath, she listened carefully, but there wasn't anything to hear that could help her determine where the horse had gone.

She looked all around. Then she noticed the old Jeep that had passed her before – and which she couldn't get out of her mind – racing along one of the several roads that cut through the fields, eventually disappearing into the bordering woods.

She assumed the driver of the Jeep was probably the owner of the horse that was roaming free. Why else would he be driving so fast and going into the woods?

When she heard a distant neigh in about the same direction, she started to jog again. She hoped the driver would see her and stop so that she could tell him, or show him, where she had last seen the horse. She was sure he'd be very glad to hear that.

*

The young woman was completely out of breath when she discovered the Jeep parked between the trees. However, the driver was nowhere to be seen. Instead, she saw a dilapidated horse trailer, which was hidden from sight between an old cabin and the slope behind it.

Rolanda didn't think anything about it at the time. After all, if someone wanted to catch his horse he had to bring it back home somehow. She became skeptical, however, when she approached the cabin and heard a tormented whinny coming from inside.

Concerned, she looked around for anyone who might know what was going on.

"Hello! Is someone here?" she yelled loudly, but there was no one there to answer.

*

When Sharazan heard the voice of his beloved former owner from inside his dark prison, he gathered all his remaining strength to try to escape. He leaned against the old boards with all his weight, but, strangely, they didn't break. When he realized that he would not be able to free himself alone, he neighed loudly into the darkness and then listened hard.

Was Rolanda really here?

She was! Once she was certain that the horse's call was coming from inside the closed shed, she ran to the door, unbolted the latch, and tore the door open.

Horrified, she saw the gelding in his prison.

"Sharazan!" she whispered, turning pale. "How did you get here?"

In three steps she was beside him. She stroked his sweaty coat and untied the rope so that he could stretch his neck.

Rolanda glanced around the narrow, confined area.

"Someone must have been very afraid of you, if he put you in such a small space. Hmmm it's going to take a while, sweetie, before I can get you out of there. Wait a minute, I'm going to look for a bucket and a water spigot. You look like you haven't had a drink for hours. What a

126

cruel thing to do! Well, if I find the man responsible for putting you in here, let me tell you, he'll be sorry!"

Sharazan listened intently to what she was saying and, because she had always treated him well and with kindness, he trusted her, even in this terrible situation. He was sure she would free him soon.

*

As Rolanda came around the corner of the cabin looking for water, the fat, bald-headed man who had tried to buy Sharazan at the circus auction was standing right in front of her.

She stopped dead and muffled a scream. She suddenly realized why the Jeep had looked so familiar.

"Oh, look, our little circus lady is trying to get her horse back. Tsk, tsk, tsk," he said, shaking his head and walking toward her. He was so close that she could smell the garlic on his breath.

Disgusted, she turned her head away, but she didn't let the man, who was leering at her, out of her sight for a second.

As soon as she had recovered from the surprise of seeing him there, she said slowly and with determination, "I'm going to get my horse out of there right now." Of course, she had no idea how she was going to do that.

Warily she took a step backward.

"Is that so?" the man opposite her said with contempt, and took another step toward her. "May I inform you, dear lady, that the horse is no longer yours!"

"And it was never yours!" she countered in a firm voice, although her knees felt weaker by the second.

"Yeah, yeah. Okay!" the bald man answered. Then, looking past Rolanda, he snapped his fingers and made a commanding gesture with his head.

"C'mon, what're you waiting for?" he asked over Rolanda's shoulder. But before she could turn around to see whom the man was talking to, she felt a dull blow to the back of her head and was pitched into blackness. She fell to the ground like a sack of potatoes.

"It's time for us to get away from here," the bald man said while his accomplice bent down, grabbed Rolanda under the arms, and dragged her into the cabin.

*

"Hey, I think I've found something," Caroline called to the others, who were all bent over, inspecting the surface of the meadow surrounding the paddock.

"It looks like a piece of a car's taillight," she added loudly, picking it up

"Isn't the blinker on your tractor broken?" Margaret Bates asked her husband. He hurried over to look at the piece of red plastic that Caroline was inspecting more closely.

"Blinker lights are orange. Taillights are red, and none of the lights on my tractor are broken!" he said. "I'd say this is a fragment from a special taillight – one from an animal transporter."

Curious now, he began looking on the ground around where Caroline had found the first piece, and discovered more fragments of red plastic a few feet away, near the base of a small tree.

"Well, someone must have rolled backward by accident and hit the tree."

"I think we should tell Gordon, now," said Marcus. "It should be possible to find an animal transporter with a broken taillight, shouldn't it?"

Carlotta nodded. "I'll drive back and phone him. Maybe you'll find something else that's of interest in the meantime. This is proof that the horses didn't leave the paddock voluntarily."

As fast as she could, she limped back to her car and let herself sink down on the driver's seat, very satisfied. Her detection skills had not disappointed her.

She stepped on the gas and was soon on the road to the Sulais' house, where Jake was watching all of the activity with binoculars.

\*

Diablo worked his way carefully down the slope. Back on level ground, he started to trot, but with each step he limped a little on his left hind leg.

From time to time he stopped, whinnied loudly, and waited for Sharazan's answer, which always came and led him in the right direction.

He kept going, driven by his instinct to find his missing friend and stablemate.

\*

Ben Kramer was just turning his hay on the meadow. He happened to glance out of the side window of his tractor and noticed Diablo descending the slope below the ruins of the old water tower.

He observed him for a moment to see which direction he was going before he jumped down from his vehicle, detached the hay baler from his tractor, and drove home as quickly as possible.

"Someone's going to be awful happy about this," he thought aloud as he ran to the telephone.

"Are you home already?" his wife, Alice, asked surprised, as Ben rushed down the hallway.

"No," he said. "Actually I'm on my way out."

While he hastily dialed Dave Bates' number and drummed impatiently on the counter with his fingers, he said, "I saw the horse."

"What horse?"

"The one the two girls were asking about this morning. They thought it had been stolen, but it's trotting happily around the old water tower."

"You didn't tell me about that," Alice said.

"I forg – Oh, hello Margaret, I – darn, that stupid answering machine!" Ben hung up. "They aren't home. What should I do now? Hmm, do you know the name of the family who moved into the Miller house?" he asked his wife. Alice shrugged her shoulders. She didn't know.

"Wait a minute," she suddenly brightened. "I think it's Solen or Sully . . . something like that."

Ben had already dialed the number for information, since there wouldn't be a listing for Ricki's family yet in the phonebook. After a short search, he got the right number.

"I hope someone's at home there, at least. If this keeps up, the animal will be miles away already."

*

"What? I understand. Okay. Thanks so much for the information. We'll drive there right now. I hope we're in luck and Diablo is still nearby. Thank you. Good-bye!"

130

Carlotta was just about to pick up the receiver and call the police station when the farmer called. She wanted to talk to Officer Gordon about the broken taillight, then decided to also tell him what she had just learned about Diablo. But when she called, he wasn't there.

Jake was very excited when she told him that Diablo had been seen again. He prayed that nothing would happen to his dear horse on his excursion through the area.

*

Carlotta drove like lightning back to the paddock meadow. She was already honking the horn before she even got to the others.

When she reached them, she leaned out of the window, waved excitedly and called out, "Quick, quick! Come! I know where Diablo is!"

"Hurray!" Ricki yelled, and ran to the car as fast as she could.

"Hey, wait for us!" Her friends tried to catch up with Ricki, but she was way ahead of them.

*Diablo! He's been seen!* He's alive! thought Ricki, her heart beating wildly as she reached the car door.

*God, please let him come home to me!* she prayed silently as she fell onto the passenger seat and rocked back and forth in excitement.

"Hurry up! Hurry up!" she called nervously to Lillian, Kevin, and Cathy, who were just now climbing into the back seat.

"We'll follow you in our car," they heard Ricki's father say, and Carlotta waved to show that she had understood. She waited with the motor running until she saw Brigitte,

131

Marcus, and Caroline, as well as Margaret and Dave get into their cars. Then she took off like a rocket.

For Ricki, the waiting seemed endless. She was afraid they would arrive too late again, and that Diablo would have changed his direction. The horrible thought that her horse could run onto the nearby highway and be hit by a car made her sick with worry.

*I wish we could fly,* she thought, but Carlotta was driving faster than the speed limit already.

When the ruins of the old water tower cam into view, she felt ice-cold waves along her spine. She began to shiver and felt like she was going to throw up.

Lillian and Cathy looked out the window and concentrated on finding the horse.

Kevin, on the other hand, who was sitting between the two girls, stared straight ahead. In the last few hours he had become very quiet. At least they had received a few clues about Diablo being nearby. But there was absolutely no news about Sharazan, and he feared that he would never see him again. As happy as he was for Ricki that she would soon have Diablo back in his stall, and as glad as he was that Diablo was okay, he was still very worried about his own horse. While the two girls kept talking and imagining where Diablo could be, behind which trees or after which curve they might discover him, Kevin's eyes began to burn. Tears of desperation ran silently down his cheeks and his shoulders began to shake.

Lillian and Cathy didn't even notice him in their excitement, but Carlotta saw him in the rearview mirror and felt an overwhelming sadness for him. She pressed her lips together tightly. She could identify with Ricki's friend all too well.

132

"Young man, stop crying!" she said, a bit too brusquely to hide her own feelings. "The world is beautiful, the sun is shining, we're on Diablo's trail – and we're going to find your Sharazan too. I promise you."

Carlotta knew that it was a risky promise, but when she saw how lovingly Ricki reached out her hand to Kevin, Carlotta swore that she would do everything in her power to find both of the horses, so that Ricki and Kevin would be happy again.

"Even if I have to drive to the ends of the earth, we are going to find Diablo and Sharazan," she repeated her promise, and then turned into the woods that Ben Kramer had described on the phone. The same woods where Rolanda had been on the trail of the driver of the old Jeep.

*

*That just can't be true,* Hank Gordon thought. He was also on his way to the same location, having just gotten a call on his cell phone from his colleagues at the police station, who informed him of Carlotta's call.

"I bet that's the same crazy women driver," he mumbled angrily when he saw a big cloud of dust in front of him.

Two other cars followed the Mercedes a few yards behind and only a little slower.

"I think I'll ask for a transfer," Gordon sighed. There was nothing else he could do but to accelerate so that he didn't lose them. He supposed that Carlotta knew exactly where she was going. After all, she drove straight into the woods as though she was hot on the trail of treasure and had to get there first, not as though she were just looking for a horse.

*

After Rolanda had been carried into the shed unconscious, Sharazan became more panicked than before. He whinnied nonstop and kept kicking against the boards, making a tremendous racket.

Max Brady paced back and forth nervously in front of the shed, fanning himself with his dirty, sweat-stained hat. Meanwhile his lame accomplice sat on the large boulder and angrily opened another bottle of beer and drank it down.

The unscrupulous animal-owner-turned-horse-thief told him once again how little he respected him.

"Don't drink so much, you still have to drive!" he snapped. "I should have listened to Joe. He said from the beginning that you weren't the man for the job!" he added, and gave the seated man a dirty look.

"I don't give a darn what you think," the man responded. He was worried because the swelling of his knee had gotten worse. It was so swollen that he almost couldn't bend his leg anymore.

"I have to do something to relieve the pain," he said, and reached for another beer.

"Stop drinking, I said!" Brady knocked the bottle out of his hand, the beer splashing all over the man's face, neck, and hands, before the bottle fell and emptied the remainder of its contents on the ground.

"Hey – are you crazy?" he yelled. He got up awkwardly; the hate for the other man was plain to see in his eyes.

Brady just looked at him with complete disdain.

"See, you can't even drink…and you can't keep that nag quiet either!" he taunted. "What can you do? Huh? You loser!"

That was the last straw. Enraged, the man bent over and picked up a fist-sized rock.

"You'll never call me a loser again, you hear me? Never again!" he hissed threateningly. But before Brady could answer, an inhuman scream filled the air. Both men spun around, frightened.

What they saw horrified them! And with a loud thud, the rock fell to the ground.

# Chapter 9

Diablo reached the woods without mishap. Sharazan's calls for help sounded as if they were coming from somewhere near, so he used the sound to get his bearings.

Diablo began to trot slowly and cautiously in the direction of the roan's neighs, careful about where he stepped, as the ground in the woods was covered with thick moss that hid roots and tree stumps that could be obstacles in his path. Frequently he would have to lower his head to avoid low-hanging branches that otherwise would have struck him in the face. Finally he reached the path in the woods, and from then on it was much easier going.

One last time the black horse stopped and listened to Sharazan's panicked whinny. In an effort to aid his stablemate, Diablo galloped forward. He no longer felt tired or thirsty, although he had suffered from thirst all day. The muggy heat had become unimportant, and his injured hind leg and sprained ankles no longer hindered him as he pressed onward. He increased his stride with all the strength left in him.

His heart was furiously pumping the blood throughout his body, and his head had begun to throb even before he rounded the last curve and saw the shed in which Sharazan fought for his freedom.

Abruptly Diablo came to a stop.

In a matter of seconds he had analyzed the situation and had recognized a scent that had filled him with anger for as long as he could remember And he knew that the moment for revenge had come. Now he would have his chance to deal with the person who had badly mistreated him and his fellow animals...the person who was also responsible for Sharazan's suffering in this prison as well as his own suffering during this whole terrible day.

Oh, how he hated this man! He had hoped never to see him again, but there he was, standing in front of the shed with another man, with no idea what was about to happen to him.

Diablo inhaled this unpleasant scent again and scraped his hoof back and forth, as though he were trying to decide what to do. But as he heard Sharazan's call for help once more, he tensed every muscle, pulled his ears back flat on his head, screamed in rage, and raced toward the two men, rearing up in front of them. He kept rearing up and driving them back toward the shed.

Then Diablo switched his attention to the man who limped – the one he has hated since he was a colt. He wanted him to feel the same fear, the same pain he had felt when the man had kicked and beat him.

Diablo came dangerously close to him and tried to force the frightened man into a corner by appearing to try to bite him. Enraged, the black horse bared his teeth and his eyes gleamed insanely. He kicked out his enemy with his front legs and the man lost his balance, falling backward in a heap, his arms above his head for protection.

137

Max Brady had seen enough. This black horse seemed to be the reincarnation of the devil himself, and while the horse focused on the other man, Brady slowly distanced himself one step at a time. When he heard the sound of cars coming closer, he tried to get to his Jeep to escape without being seen. Ignoring the screams of his partner, he ran and reached the safety of his Jeep just as the parade of cars came into view.

\*

When Carlotta, who was in the lead, rounded the curve in the forest path, Ricki called out, "My God! Up there...Diablo! Good grief, what's he doing? He's going to kill him that man!"

Even before the Mercedes had come to a complete stop, she had opened the passenger door and jumped out. Her friends weren't far behind.

"Diablo! Diablo! No! Don't!" Ricki's voice screamed in panic as she ran toward her horse.

But should she dare to go close to him or would he attack her as well?

\*

In the meantime, Carlotta discovered Brady trying to flee. Like a stunt drive in a crime movie, she immediately stepped on the gas and drove directly in front of the Jeep, blocking his escape. Brady had parked his vehicle in front of two huge evergreens, so he couldn't make his getaway by driving in reverse either.

Within minutes Marcus and Dave arrived and quickly assessed the situation. They got out of their cars and ran over to the Jeep, positioning themselves in front of both doors, so that Brady couldn't get out.

As Carlotta awkwardly exited her car and was making her way to the Jeep, Brigitte saw Ricki a few feet away from the enraged Diablo and screamed.

"My God, Marcus! Do something! Ricki –"

Margaret and Caroline, both pale with fear and worry, ran over to her. Neither had ever seen a horse behave this wildly before.

Marcus turned around at his wife's outcry. He had noticed Diablo's behavior in front of the shed as he was driving up, but had failed to see the man cringing on the ground in front of the horse. He also hadn't seen Ricki approaching her horse. Now he did.

"Ricki – no!" he yelled and ran toward her.

At that moment he didn't care about Brady anymore. He was scared to death for his daughter.

The animal trainer saw his opportunity immediately and jumped out of the car, but he hadn't reckoned with Carlotta.

Just as Hank Gordon was bringing his Volvo to a screeching halt on the gravel path, Carlotta managed to trip Brady with her crutch. Before the man could get up, Lillian's father knelt on top of him, holding him down with his knees.

Gordon raced toward the two men, unfastening his handcuffs along the way. Two seconds later he snapped them around the wrists of the infamous animal trainer.

"I'm innocent," Brady claimed at once, and jerked his head in the direction of the shed. "That man over there stole a horse and beat a woman. I was just on my way to the police, but these people wouldn't let me go," he lied.

139

Gordon paid him no attention and just stared at the horrible scene Diablo was making.

*

Ricki stood a few yards away from Diablo, unable to move, as she heard her father's warning shout.

In her mind she saw her horse as he laid his head lovingly on her shoulder and looked trustingly into her eyes. She saw herself asleep beside him in his stall. She recalled how Diablo had broken down the door to the riding academy during the fire and saved Jake and the other horses. Her horse was the most wonderful horse in the world. Right then and there she knew Diablo would never do anything to hurt her; the love between them could never turn to hate.

Ricki took in a deep breath and slowly exhaled, feeling the tenseness leave her body.

"Diablo! Hey, Diablo, my boy, come here," she said, loud enough so that he could hear her but not loud enough to scare him even more. She raised her hand and moved cautiously in his direction.

"Ricki! Come back immediately!"

"That's too dangerous!"

"Don't do anything stupid. Leave him alone. That's not the Diablo you know!"

She could barely hear the pleas of her parents and friends. It was as though they were behind a thick cloud. She just kept walking toward her horse.

Meantime, Carlotta had reached Marcus were pulling him back. At the same time, she indicated to the others that they should be quiet.

"Let her alone!" she whispered sharply to Ricki's father. "She knows what she's doing. If anyone can calm that

140

horse down, it's her. Believe me, I know horses, he won't hurt her."

"I hope Diablo knows that too," whispered Marcus hoarsely, and reluctantly held back.

Time seemed to stand still; all eyes were on Ricki.

She shut out everything and everyone around her except Diablo. She visualized they were in the middle of a huge meadow full of wildflowers. She could hear the birds, watch the butterflies as they danced from blossom to blossom, and she looked proudly at her wonderful black horse galloping joyfully across the meadow toward her.

Ricki laughed and stretched out her hand to him. She knew he would stop in time so as not to hurt her.

"You are the most beautiful horse in the world," she called to him. As though he wanted to prove this to her, he came down on his hind legs and reared up in front of her.

"Wow! That's super! Do that again! You look so great doing that, do you know that?"

Ricki's voice was full of admiration, and after Diablo had reared up again to his full height, his owner said forcefully, "That's enough now! Let's go home!" And she grabbed his bridle, stroked his neck, and whispered lovingly in his ear, "You're a good boy! You are a wonderful horse, sweetie, but come, now!"

Then Ricki led her horse, who was soaking wet with sweat, as though nothing had happened.

Only when she had distanced herself a few yards from the shed, did she see the crouching man, who was so frightened that he couldn't move a muscle. Then she glanced at Diablo, who stood beside her as peacefully as a lamb, enjoying her stroking him, and wondered what had happened here to cause his frenzied behavior.

As the reality of the last few minutes began to sink in, Ricki's legs started to tremble. She had no idea how she had managed to grab the bridle of the wild horse and how close she came to being hurt.

After Ricki had led the horse away, Margaret Bates and Ricki's father approached the man cringing in front of the shed. Carefully they helped him lie down and then checked him all over for injuries, but the only thing they could find was the hugely swollen knee.

"Well, that's nothing compared to what could have happened," Marcus said, relieved. Only seconds later, however, he and Margaret exchanged surprised glances as they realized that the knee had already been bandaged. It must have been an old injury.

*

Brigitte was still rooted in the same spot, in a state of shock. She couldn't believe what she had just seen.

Caroline Thomas stood next to her with her arm around Brigitte's shoulder. She had had a lot of experience with horses while living with her ex-husband, and she was very impressed with Ricki's courageous intervention.

"Diablo is a wonderful and loving horse," she said, trying to comfort Brigitte. "I don't know why he attacked that man over there, but I am convinced there was a reason."

Brigitte stared at Diablo. "That loving horse could have killed my daughter!"

Caroline nodded. "That's right. Any horse could kill a person if it wanted to, but Diablo didn't hurt Ricki or that man, and that means your 'devil' isn't really a devil!"

Brigitte knew that Caroline was right, but at the moment

she wasn't willing to approach Diablo with the same trust she had before. Her fears for Ricki were still too great.

Caroline, a mother herself, understood Brigitte's feelings. She gave her another hug and then stepped aside. She sensed that Brigitte needed a moment to herself to come to grips with all that she had seen and heard.

*

With the crisis over, Lillian, Cathy, and Kevin rushed to Ricki's side and, one after the other, they hugged her and Diablo. It was clear that Diablo was enjoying their attention. He liked being the center of attention because that meant he usually got some treats, or at least a lot of stroking.

"I bet you're glad that you have him back," Cathy said with shining eyes, and Lillian laughed away her tenseness as well.

"Man, I am so happy for you, I can't tell you how much! By the way, that was some performance back there. I don't know if I could have done that if it had been Holli standing there like that in front of me!"

"Well," said Ricki, her hand still around her horse's neck, "I'm not sure I could do it again. At that moment I just wasn't thinking about how wild with rage Diablo was. I imagined him rearing up like that in joy, like he does all the time in the paddock, and suddenly I wasn't afraid of him anymore."

"Hey, that was really cool! I thought he was going to smash your head in. Looking at him now, the last few minutes seem like a nightmare, don't they?" Cathy said, gazing at the horse with amazement as he scraped at the gravel with his hoof.

"I think I should dry him off," Ricki said, a lump in her throat. She still didn't know if this sudden, uncharacteristic behavior of Diablo's would have long-term consequences for him.

*

Kevin leaned against Diablo and nuzzled his face in the mane of the first horse he had ridden since Leonardo's death.

"You good horse. It's so great to have you back," he said quietly. He was genuinely happy that Diablo had been found, but Ricki knew exactly what her friend was thinking and she whispered in his ear: "Remember what Carlotta said in the car. We're going to find Sharazan too, even if we have to search the ends of the earth!"

Kevin nodded sadly and stepped aside so that Ricki could take her horse to be rubbed down, but Diablo had no intention of going with his owner.

He raised his head abruptly, began to whinny shrilly and to dance restlessly around Ricki.

"Oh, no, my darling, not again!"

Ricki tried to turn the horse away so that he couldn't see her father and Dave Bates as they helped the stranger up. She had assumed that Diablo would attack the man again if he saw him standing and wanted to prevent that at all costs. But Marcus and Dave walked him to one of the cars, where they settled him in the back seat. Officer Gordon had phoned for medical assistance, and they wanted the injured man to be as comfortable as possible until the doctor arrived.

But when the answering neigh to Diablo's call resounded from the old woodshed, everyone stopped what they were doing and listened, riveted.

"My God, am I dreaming or was that another horse?" Hank Gordon broke the silence. He was still holding onto Brady, who was struggling to get away, and waiting for his colleagues to arrive and take the animal trainer to the police station for questioning.

"Sharazan?" whispered Kevin tonelessly, and then startled everyone by shouting. "It's Sharazan! Those guys locked him in there!"

He ran to the shed, Cathy and Lillian right behind him, and Caroline and Carlotta following them as fast as Carlotta's handicap allowed.

*

Sharazan had not made a sound throughout the entire episode with Diablo. He had listened intently in the darkness and hoped that the door would be opened soon.

Now that all was relatively quiet again, he heard Diablo's whinny, and he began to kick with all his might against the walls of his prison, as he had done previously.

Kevin ripped open the shed door, falling backward with the force of his pull. The smell of horse urine made him sick to his stomach. He coughed and tried to conquer his nausea. When he saw his beloved horse, his eyes filled with love. Nothing else mattered. He ran over to him, took his head in his arms, and closed his eyes. Tears of overwhelming happiness rolled down his cheeks and fell onto the forehead of the exhausted animal.

"It's him! I have him back! Sharazan, my best friend, I am so happy I have you back! Dear God, thank you so much. Thank you, thank you, thank you!"

145

Kevin could hardly believe his luck. It was as though the horse of his dreams had been given to him twice.

Thankful, he smiled at Carlotta with gratitude, embarrassed by his tears, and she came to him and gave him a big hug.

"See, I told you. You should believe an old woman."

Kevin, happy to agree with the former circus performer, nodded and gave her a kiss on the cheek.

"Thank you for not giving up and for driving us all around. I will never, never forget that!" he said with such earnest sincerity that Carlotta had to laugh.

"I'll remind you that you said that. You can be sure of it!"

*

Lillian and Cathy had also entered the narrow shed with Caroline. While Kevin's mother hugged him, relieved and happy. The two girls inspected the tight space trying to figure out the best way of getting Sharazan out of there.

Suddenly Lillian screamed.

"Someone is lying over there," she pointed, "in the corner!"

Cathy was the first to reach her.

"This is unbelievable! It's Rolanda from the circus!"

Caroline let go of Kevin and pushed the girls quickly aside. She hurried to the young woman who was lying unconscious, bound and gagged like a piece of rubbish, on the floor of the stinking shed.

*

Right after Lillian's scream, Hank Gordon appeared in the doorway. A police car had arrived a few minutes before and the two officers took the resisting Brady to the police station.

When Gordon saw Rolanda, he immediately took out his cell phone and called for additional emergency medical backup. Then he hurried over to Caroline, who had already removed the gag and ropes that bound Rolanda.

"I got to the EMS just as they were leaving to come here. They're sending an ambulance. The doctor and the emergency team should be here in a few minutes." He put his finger on Rolanda's jugular vein and breathed a sigh of relief.

"Thank God, she's alive.

Caroline stared at the policeman with consternation. "What kind of a person does something like this?" she asked softly.

Gordon didn't answer her question directly. He just said, "I have the feeling that a lot of things are connected to this horse theft."

Together they picked the woman up and carried her outside to the fresh air, where a few seconds later, still in shock, she opened her eyes.

Her lips formed the word "Sharazan," and Caroline smiled and nodded to her to calm her.

"He's fine! Stay quiet. The doctor will be here any minute now!"

Rolanda understood and closed her eyes again. She didn't even notice that soon after she was put onto a gurney and carried to the ambulance.

The injured man was also taken to the nearby hospital. Hank Gordon planned to go there later and question him.

*

147

Kevin was still standing beside his horse, delirious with joy. Now that the boy was with him, Sharazan waited patiently in the shed for another half hour, until Marcus and Dave were able to free him.

*

"So, what did you find out about everything?" Ricki asked Officer Gordon a few days later as everyone gathered around the Sulais' picnic table watching the horses at home in the paddock. They were all curious about the outcome of the police investigation.

"Well," the policeman began, taking the piece of freshly baked marble cake Brigitte offered him, "Brady was so scared that he confessed almost immediately to being involved in several animal thefts prior to this one. Now he will be held accountable. He had planned to steal both circus horses and sell them to a large circus abroad, with which he had already made an agreement. By the way, the broken taillight you found near the paddock belongs to Brady's horse trailer."

"How's Rolanda?" Cathy wanted to know.

"She's doing as well as can be expected. When she found out that her own husband was involved in the horse theft and that it was him who had beaten her so brutally, she told her father to start divorce proceedings in her name."

"What?! Piotr was the one who beat up Rolanda? That means he was the one Diablo attacked! Boy, have I been a complete idiot! I should have recognized him. After all, I was at the circus for several days!" Cathy clenched her fists and shook her head, angry with herself.

148

Officer Gordon just grinned. "Piotr my foot! His real name is Chris Hinkley and he – "

"What?!" Jake jumped up. "Did you say Chris Hinkley? And there's no doubt?"

"That's right," Gordon answered, looking at Jake questioningly.

"Well, then I can understand why Diablo went wild."

Then Jake told Hank Gordon and everyone else present about the incident on the Summersfield Ranch that he'd told Ricki some time back.

When it became clear why Diablo reacted so violently when he was around Hinkley, Brigitte wholeheartedly forgave her daughter's horse.

"Caroline was right when she said Diablo had a reason for acting crazy like that. But I didn't believe her because I didn't think a horse was capable of such emotional reactions, but now…"

Ricki stood up and gave her mother a big hug. "Does that mean that you'll finally go with me to his stall and wish Diablo good night with a few carrots?"

Brigitte nodded. "I guess so. I have to ask him to forgive me," she laughed.

"What about the motorcyclists who chased Diablo? Were they ever found?" Lillian wanted to know.

"No, unfortunately, not yet. Since we don't have their license plate numbers and the three of them are completely unknown in town, we think it'll be very difficult to find them, especially since no one at the Red Moon Café can remember seeing them. Besides, they're probably long gone by now. And, speaking of license plates…" Hank Gordon added, looking directly at Carlotta. "Due to the fact that you brought this horse thief down and, therefore, have done us a huge service, I've decided to forget about the ticket for speeding – but only if you promise me never again to drive that fast within any speed limit!"

Carlotta gave him a charming smile from across the table.

"And you, young man," she chided the officer, "from now on you should devote your free time to catching horse thieves instead of following old women who have to speed to escape from you."

"She just can't let it alone!" Gordon chuckled, getting up to leave. He touched his cap in a gesture of farewell and said good-bye, thanking them all for their help.

Ricki started to follow the officer then turned to her friends. "Come on," she said, "let's go to the paddock and see if all the animals are still there."

"But you can see that from here," Carlotta replied.

"I just want to make sure," she answered, laughing, and, with Harry in the lead, they ran to the horses and Chico, who was already greeting his friend Harry with a loud hee-haw.

"Oh, life is so wonderful," shouted Ricki, and pirouetted in happiness, while back in the house, Brigitte inspected the sugar bowl. "Oh, that girl! That little thief of a daughter just stole all my sugar cubes!"

But when she saw how joyously Ricki hugged her Diablo, she was just thankful that the horse was back home and her daughter was at peace again.

As she cheerfully added more sugar cubes to the bowl, Brigitte smiled to herself. "Who cares if the sugar bowl has to be refilled every day!"